It is a very interesting book about cute cats. During those cats' adventures, I actually felt that I was inside of the cats' mind, learn and think of love, freedom and faith. Also, I learned lots of information about world of cats.
I want to have a cat.

> Julia (Seung-ah Han)
> 한승아, 12 years old
> Seoul, Korea

I love adventures of Rascal and his friends in the Enchanted Forest

> Camila S age:11
> Coquitlam, Canada

I never heard before about Prehistoric Mouse. I love the idea of meeting of cats from different countries.

> Michael, 10 years old
> Barcelona, Spain

A cat's story, with a cat's perspective and his wild adventures that makes you wonder "what do cats really think about? and what do they do all day?
This is a fascinating story, and a lot of exciting adventures yet to be told...

> By Joanna Maczynska Age 16
> Vancouver, Canada

A book for kids??? – No!!! Who said that his book was only for children? I am an adult (65 years old) and I still enjoy reading it. The positive energy just jumps out of those pages. There are plenty of interesting ideas. I've read it from cover to cover and I'm looking forward to reading more stories about Rascal and his companions.

*Captain Pawel N.*

"Why Some Cats are Rascals?" is a must read for everyone. Rascal will touch your soul and heart. A great idea is to donate this book to a sick child at your local hospital. This may be the best gift you offer to that child.

*Diana K. (25 years old)*

"Why some cats are Rascals" has it all... A book that tells both a story that challenges a child's imagination as well as teaches them a lesson or two about "real life" and problems they must learn to deal with. Compassion, love, understanding others – these are some of the values your child will learn from this book.

*Teresa (mother of a 10 years old daughter)*

This book could easily become an animated movie. If that happens, I'll be first in line.

*Tom (22 year old)*

I'd call it a page-turner. I commend the author for writing a story that educate while being a fun read at the same time; and most importantly, for teaching our children such good values as friendship, compassion, love, etc. while staying away from ever-so-popular nowadays violence.

*Jan, 44*

The characters are realistic. They live with me in a white wooden house with a big garden and a view of mountains. Their names are real too. However, some of them – like Grandma Calico and Uncle Toothless – are now on the other side of the rainbow...

I am dedicating this book to all cats and veterinarians from Cat-anada and all around the world.

*Boszenna Nowiki, the author*

## *Cat Trivia*

How many cats are there in the world?
How many hours a day does a cat sleep?
Are cats more popular in America than dogs?

The answers are... somewhere in the book.

# Why Some Cats are Rascals

## Book 1

Boszenna Nowiki

Healthy Life Press Inc.

Text copyright © 2005 by Boszenna Nowiki


Cover and illustration copyright © 2005 by Healthy Life Press Inc.


Cover designed by Luke Zukowski
Illustrations by Joanna Maczynska


Published by:
Healthy Life Press Inc.
1733 H Street Suite 330 PMB 860
Blaine,Wa 98230   USA
Tel. 1 (888) 575-3173
info@netinfodirect.com
www.netinfodirect.com

First Edition.


ISBN 978-0-9727328-2-6
LCCN 2005928184


Printed and bound in Poland by
Drukarnia Wydawnictw Naukowych Sp. z o.o., Łódź

# Part 1

# Quest for Freedom

Rascal was sitting on the windowsill, watching the rain. His eyes lazily followed the drops as they fell from the gray sky. The soft cat song he was humming was the only sound in the quiet attic. There wasn't much light either. Two small windows facing the north side barely chased away the darkness, and long shadows cast odd shapes on the bare wooden walls. Rascal peered through the rain-soaked window at the mountains that loomed in the distance, half hidden in thick clouds. He had gazed at them so many times before, but he had never ventured off that far.

He sighed deeply and said, "Starting today, I'm writing a diary."

Lumby, a three-month old white and black kitten with long hair and two black hearts on the back of his white feet, leaped off the box he was sitting on and sat in front of Rascal, looking up at him curiously. "What's a diary?" he asked.

"You will see! All of you I will blacken!"

Lumby took a step backwards, scared by Rascal's little joke.

Rascal smiled and continued, "A diary is a memoir, a work of art in which every day portrays only truth and more truth. If I forget the truth, I will invent it, but truth it will always be." He smiled slyly and jumped into the third drawer of a five-drawer white cabinet.  Cracking open a small leather diary, Rascal fetched his pen and began to write.

*This morning I looked in the mirror and was amazed at how Nature gave so much beauty in one body...in a few words I will introduce myself. I'm amazingly beautifully orange on the nose and my lip is full of black spots.  My name is Rascal.*

Just as he was admiring his own words, another cat, much bigger, poked his nose into the drawer where Rascal was writing.  "Hey, what are you doing there?" the fat cat asked.

It was Rascal's brother, Philosopher.  He looked at Rascal's writing and commented, "Eeeee, your writing isn't worth one pound of tuft, Rascal."

Rascal just glared at him.

Casually licking his paws, Philosopher continued, "Why don't you write this: I have a brother my age, three years old.  He is fat, his fur is grayish-blue; his collar and socks are white. His name is Philosopher and he has a white spot on his nose.  He's very slow but reads a lot and thinks even more.  Sometimes while thinking, he catches a mouse.  He has a cat's patience.  I prefer flies; they are easier to catch than mice."

Meanwhile small Lumby, with his short jumps, had left the two brothers for another part of the attic to visit with Grandma, an older calico cat. Everyone called her simply "Grandma," though

Lumby was pretty sure that wasn't her real name. He looked up at her with his big eyes and said, "Please, Grandma, tell us one of the cat legends. A funny one."

Two orange ears, a white mustache and a freckled nose peeked from the third drawer to listen. Rascal wrote:

*So, Grandma is very old; soon she'll be 22 winters. It must be some kind of a secret because I've never heard before about such an old cat.*

Grandmother stretched. Lumby could hear her bones creaking and popping. It made him a little scared, but then Grandma smiled, cleared her throat and began. "A long time ago, when I was young..."

"Grandma was young?" interrupted Lumby.

"Yes, child, and I used to love listening to the old legends too." She sighed and spoke as to herself or to the window. "The clouds in the sky were smiling at me, stars and sun came back for me every day."

Lumby waited patiently for her to continue. It was very quiet in the room. Outside the window, the dark clouds continued to hide the midday sun. But the rain seemed to pause and listen to the calico. With great melancholy, she said, "I was running with the wind, jumping and playing. That was freedom!"

"Is it true?" asked Lumby, his eyes widening in surprise.

"Grandma never lies," the old cat said in a serious

tone.

"I was thinking that," said the happy kitten, nodding his agreement.

The old calico continued. "A real cat counts only on his own strength ... and thinks somehow it will always be enough."

After those words the rest of the cats sat around Grandma. There was a five-year-old snow-white cat named Snow, and her husband Dandy, a black cat with a smattering of white under his jaw. He was fond of fashion. Also there was Sofia, a white and black cat from Poland, and Bunny, a one-year-old white and gray without a tail, which made him look like a Japanese Bobtail. And of course Lumby, who was from the country. He was always very happy, smiling, jumping and playing around. His name came from the small town where he was born, close to Kelowna, in British Columbia, Canada.

\*\*\*

Away from the others, Rascal lay curled up in his cabinet drawer, busily writing down everything. Philosopher was watching from the highest shelf close to the door. Uncle Toothless, a 14 year old cat without teeth, yellow with a white tummy and white socks, spent his time in the other parts of the house and went to the garden sometimes. The rest of the cats were closed in one north room with two windows and a view of a big mountain, named Grouse Mountain, and to the left two peaks named Sisters.

Grandma looked around at the cats gathered all about her and said, "I'm happy seeing you; soon I have to go."

"Gee!" said Lumby.

"Gee!" said the rest of the cats. "Please don't go!"

She smiled softly and Lumby jumped up and embraced her. She was not used to cats caressing and shyly said, "Watch out, you will knock me over!"

Grandma was really very happy, however, and she stealthily licked Lumby's nose.

Rascal was carefully watching the entire scene. Clutching his pen, he again began writing in his diary.

*Grandma never was like that before; it looks like something is in the air. She always beat us with her paws and never allowed us to come too close to her. Discipline was her best model of virtue. But she was different to the humans; she always was very friendly to them and wanted more petting. She would cuddle up to them and purr... Something is wrong with our Grandma.*

Grandmother was talking about "the olden days," the days of her youth. She sparked the imaginations of the younger cats with her tall tales of sleeping in the rubbish can and under the stars, about the fancy Ball that the cats used to organize two times a year, and the competitions that they once had walking on the wooden fence. She also spoke dreamily of the freedom of cats she knew, who lived in the wild. Old Grandma seemed to get more energy while talking about her younger days. "Always be very active," she warned. "There are lots of lazy cats without ambition. Their life is only to do the minimum: sleep and eat until death. That's no way to live! Listen to me, you youngsters. To be alive means to have a goal. Lots of cats have nice ideas but never use them. It is not enough just to think success or to have ideas; they must be demonstrated. So thinking success alone does not make you successful. But all actions start from your thoughts."

Lumby opened his mouth to say something, but then Grandma sighed heavily and said, "But it is also true that in the moment you decide to be successful you will encounter lots of obstacles. So remember, for real cats they are not obstacles!" She stopped and looked like she was asleep.

All the cats talked quietly amongst themselves. Grandma seemed to have fallen asleep and none of them dared to awaken her. Philosopher sat in silence with his right ear to the front and left ear to the back as he looked out the window. When the old cat opened her eyes he asked, "Do you know, my Grandma, where there are some good mouse holes close by?"

The old cat instantly seemed wide awake again. She smiled. "Yes, my son. In old houses there are incredibly gorgeous mice," she said and started licking her fur.

Philosopher scrunched up his face, a habit he had when he was curious about something. "Are those old houses somewhere close by?" he asked. This time his left ear moved to the front and his right ear moved to the back.

Grandma stretched again, and again the popping and creaking from her old bones and joints caught the other cats' attention. But she seemed not even to notice, or at least not to care. "A long time ago I knew every mouse hole," she said. "I remember when I was living in the basement of number 8. The house was clean and modern, with 6 mice holes and 1 rat hole. It also had running water in the outside gutter when it rained. It was splendidly situated, close to the forest where forest and field mice had appointments. Every Friday we got some salmon because the people living on the first floor eat fish."

"How would I find that?" Philosopher asked.

"Very easy. When you go along the wall..."

Rascal wrote every word she uttered into his diary, listening intently from the third drawer.

"May I ask Grandma about something?" Philosopher asked.

"Yes, son." (She always said son, because she had close to 100 children and lots of grandchildren).

"For a long time I have had this question. Should cats go to the dentist and veterinarian?"

Grandmother's face lit with a smile. "Thanks to

our doc, his name was…name was…, Oh! Mouse Bone! I forget his name. When I remember I will tell you. But thanks to him my arthritis is less and less problematic. He killed fleas and lice, and ear mites. I still have nice teeth," she said and showed her teeth, opening her mouth in a nice cat's smile. Then she said, "Look at Uncle Toothless, he turned 14 this spring He never goes to the vet and lately he became very querulous and only complains. Everything aches, and his fur is full of fleas quarrelling there all night long. Because he was afraid of the dentist and doctor, he is suffering now. He complains in the morning, before lunch, after dinner …when it rains, when it's sunny…when he is hungry, when he is full."

Hearing her words, Lumby jumped up and began to dance. "When I was at the vet's it was very nice," he said and almost choked from the excitement. "I tell you, guys, there were lots of cats, dogs, and other animals which I never saw in my life before; they had veeeeeryyyyyy looooong eeeeeaaaars, rabbits I think. There were also goldfish and turtles. I would have liked to play with them but the fish wanted to swim in the closed pool, and the turtle was very slow. The part I liked best was when a small girl was checking my heart. She petted every hair on my back. Oh! I want to go to that clinic, now!"

"Lumby! Don't exaggerate!" said Bunny, who was in the cats' custom a self-styled babysitter. "I was there also with you! All my legs were trembling with fear because of the strange smells but one thing

18

is true, nobody harmed us. Everybody said, 'Look at that cat without a tail, how pretty he is. What nice green eyes and how much wisdom there is in his glance.'"

"Hey, raw lads," said Rascal, laughing. "Now I want to go, I will leave my diary for later and go to the vet right now."

"Pshaw!" said Snow. "For me, going to the doc is not interesting at all. I prefer basking in the sun one hundred times more than having someone peep in my throat and teeth and…"

"I don't mind having my teeth checked as long as I don't have to open my mouth," confessed Philosopher, clenching his teeth.

"Don't clench your teeth, it is not healthy," scolded Sofia.

"In that case let's make a Ball to honor cat doctors and cat dentists," Rascal said, smiling, and jumping high. Then with one leap he jumped onto the shelf, and from the shelf to the barrel where there was dry cat food. Then he burst to the doors of the first walk-in closet and shot like an arrow to the second walk-in closet, which was opposite the first. By a stroke of good luck the doors were open; otherwise he would have turned into an orange pie on the door. With grace he jumped onto the bookcase, then with a huge jump onto the white cabinet with five drawers.

Lumby, who was still dancing on the floor, looked at the orange cat with amazement. As Rascal was flying he shouted, "This is the dance of good health, perfect feeling, agility, exercise, cleverness…"

"And healthy kidneys," added Philosopher.

"Play with us!" shouted Rascal, ready to jump on the chandelier.

Philosopher smiled and said, "I am trying to figure out one secret, on which I will think in the future. I can not understand why life is this way, when cats want it another way."

"Dance with us! Don't worry about secrets. What for?" his brother Rascal said, knowing he would never be bothered by such things.

Philosopher put his two ears back and said, loudly, "I'm too important a scholar for that. But I like to eat a lot of good food because it helps my thinking. See, my brother…"

"I like to talk too much and ask about everything," Rascal said, smiling. "Maybe if…"

"What is it you are thinking?" Philosopher said, looking at his brother suspiciously.

A serious expression came over Rascal's face. "Maybe we should go to look for freedom."

Rascal thought for a moment. "Hmm… to those old houses where there are easy and tasty mice and rats or a fat mole."

"What if we get lost somewhere?"

"I don't know, maybe something lucky will happen to us," said Rascal, with no concern at all in his voice.

Lumby had overheard all of this. He marched up to Grandma and sat before her. Innocently, the kitten asked, "Grandma, what is freedom?"

The old cat seemed amused by the question. She nuzzled the youngster's nose affectionately and then began to speak. "Freedom is a lifestyle, my boy," she said. "Winter with moonlit nights hunting for mice, an evening chase for rats, playing hide and seek with young robins who have left their nests. Dancing two times in a year. Nothing makes you feel as distinguished as being invited to a March dance where Public Cat's Company gives such a concert you will never forget. Then you dance and dance until morning. Even the highest roof is a piece of cake. Geee! THAT is freedom!"

Lumby's eyes lit up. This all sounded too good to be true. He jumped up and started to dance around Bunny.

"You are too small," Bunny said, shaking his head at the kitten.

Lumby stopped dancing for a moment. "No, I am not too little!" he protested. "I know how to write the word 'cat'... and I do it with only two errors."

Grandmother tried not to laugh at the cute little kitten. She continued. "Freedom is a state of mind, but remember, it must be balanced. Too much freedom is like too much cat food or too much sleep. You will have a stomach ache or a headache."

\*\*\*

After a supper of canned beef with carrots, the cats went to sleep, Grandma on a small wooden cupboard under the window, Philosopher in a basket on the table, Snow with Dandy on the last shelf, Bunny and Lumby in the box standing on the floor close to the bookshelf.

It was very quiet, only occasional noises made by the dreaming cats were heard. Rascal tried to sleep in the second drawer but could not. No sooner did he close his eyes, they suddenly opened again with the sound of a rustle.

"Who is that?" whispered Rascal, not wanting to wake up the rest of the cats.

"Freedom," said a very tiny voice.

At that moment Rascal opened his eyes wide and looked around, he sniffed every nook and corner. Once again he checked closed doors, peeped in every drawer, but freedom was not there...

\*\*\*

The next morning, Rascal was restless.

"How did you sleep, Brother?" asked Philosopher before breakfast.

"Not too good," growled Rascal, reluctantly.

"Why? Were mice dancing...?"

"I cannot sleep since I heard of freedom."

His brother looked at Rascal as if he had lost his mind. "What does that mean?"

"Eeeee, too much talk about that," Rascal grumbled.

Philosopher stared up at the ceiling for a while,

then said, "Freedom and free will do not exist. They are like a ghost, you can't catch them, they are invisible and cannot be touched. For example, we have free will but I cannot be a Bengal tiger if I want to be, I have to be a cat for the rest of my life. See, my brother, in contemplation this morning I have discovered that freedom does not make me free. The same with free will. If, in the name of freedom, I do whatever I want to do, I'm only a slave of freedom."

Rascal wanted to ask his brother more questions about his very important sounding—but hard to understand—words. But he didn't want to sound dumb in front of the smart one so he kept his mouth shut.

Later, Rascal was once again writing in his diary.

*Cloudy sky, cloudy... Today is another day without my darling Diana, an 11 year old girl, and 12 years old Hubert. They left us... Something they said about Sedona in Arizona where there are vortexes, where there are scorpions and snakes.*

Rascal nodded his orange colored head sadly and continued writing.

*Yes, scorpions and snakes in those vortexes are more important than Rascal, Philosopher, and all the others, and travel by plane is more important than taking care of their best pets.*

Rascal sighed. After thinking for a long time—which for Rascal was two and a half seconds—he got back to his good humor. With lots of energy and grace, he jumped out of the drawer into the middle of the room and said, "Hey. Listen, cats, I got an idea!"

"Nothing new," said Bunny, looking intently.

Sofia only nodded her head. "You have 1001 ideas in a minute," she said. "We don't want to hear about your ideas!"

Rascal didn't get mad; he was never one to take offense. He glanced at Philosopher and nodded in the direction of the closet. They both entered the closet, where they sat comfortably on the brown attaché case and whispered together. The cats heard only, "We have to do this another way. Think, Rascal, please."

"I'm thinking," Rascal said. He sat with his paws in front of him, occasionally licking them and cleaning his whiskers. Many ideas went through his head, but none of them seemed very useful. Mostly they were thoughts of mice and fish. After a while he said, "This is no good, your thoughts are better than mine."

"That is the truth!" Philosopher said and smiled, adding, "But it is necessary for us both to think."

"We will think, then," Rascal said, nodding in agreement.

The two cats sat side by side on top of the brown attaché case. Occasionally one would lick the other's back, a sign of affection among cats. They even nodded off for a catnap once or twice. They thought for a long time. They had hundreds of ideas… but not one idea that stood out from the others.

*** 

At dinner that evening, Rascal jumped suddenly as if he had been bitten by a scorpion, barely missing their bowl of water. "I have!..."

"Tell us! What have you found?" the others replied in unison.

Rascal looked around, then tilted his head to Philosopher's ear and whispered for a long time. Philosopher listened with care, nodded three times and said with respect, "Yes, this we should do. That is a very wise idea," and finished licking up the few drops of water left in the bowl.

"Let's go! Let's tell our idea to the rest of the cats," said Rascal gleefully.

But Grandma raised her head. Their enthusiasm was halted in its tracks. "Quiet, I want to sleep, I feel sick today. That last can of salmon must not have agreed with my stomach." She lowered her head onto her front paws and swished her long tail back and forth. Her eyes slowly closed.

The other cats became very quiet, walking softly on their padded feet. From time to time whispering could be heard from the corners, "Maybe it is okay to try it?"

"If you are not afraid, try it, but I'm afraid."

"Me too. I'm afraid but I will try."

As the cats were muttering amongst themselves, the front door opened with a creak. A tall boy with short blond hair entered. It was 15 year old Tom. He smiled at the cats and said, "I'm here today and I will be here for a week to feed you guys for your young masters, Diana and Hubert." Then, not waiting for a response, he started to clean their bowls and get fresh water from the tap and food from the bag in the pantry.

Grandmother, as usual, came to Tom and rubbed against his legs, purring, asking for a caress.

"Do you see? I told you," growled Rascal to his brother. Then to the calico he said, "Grandma, we would like to go outside for a moment, just for a minute or two. We would like to breathe the fresh air from the garden and feel what freedom might be like. We want to look at the pigeons too with our naked eyes instead of through the window." He watched as Grandma continued rubbing her body against Tom's leg, trying to get noticed.

The calico was very busy purring. She nodded her head, giving permission for them to go outside. The door was open a little, and the cats trotted to the corridor without being noticed, then down the stairs to the front door, their tails waving back and forth with excitement. Rascal jumped on the door handle and the door opened even wider onto the backyard.

On the way to freedom they came upon Uncle Toothless, lying in a patch of pale sunlight on the carpet. He looked surprised and asked, "Where are you going?"

"We are going to look for freedom," Rascal meowed proudly.

"Come with us, Uncle Toothless," Lumby said joyfully, touching the end of Uncle's tail.

"Don't touch my tail!" Uncle snapped angrily. "I'm staying right here."

"Okay, see you," said the cats.

"Take care and don't go too far. There are many strange and unfriendly creatures outside," said Uncle and started carefully licking his tail. "I won't be surprised to see all of you running back here in panic before too long!"

The cats figured their grouchy old uncle was just trying to scare them with his warnings. They soon put his words out of their minds as they marched to the green hedge at the edge of the yard. They were too excited to be scared. The edge of the yard was connected to the neighbor's rose garden, and the cats scampered along and disappeared inside. They had never ventured this far before. Past the hedge it was an unknown territory.

\*\*\*

Back inside the house, Tom found out what happened and called Diana and Hubert on his cell-phone. "Listen, guys! The cats got outside and went to the garden."

27

"Don't worry. Nothing big," Hubert replied.

Tom wasn't sure what he meant.

"They sometimes go to the garden," Hubert explained. "Look out the door tomorrow and you'll see how tame they'll be and how willingly they'll come inside. And don't forget that Uncle Toothless has no teeth so he eats only raw ground meat."

"I remember," said Tom, thinking, *"That's strange. They've never done this to me before."*

"And Grandma?" Diana asked.

"Grandma! I was petting Grandma. She is always the first to come to me and wants to be petted all the time," Tom said confidently.

"Don't worry. Grandma likes solitude. She will be very happy alone. And those rascals better sleep in the garden. Tomorrow look for them and you will see how patiently they will be waiting at the door."

\*\*\*

While Tom was talking to Diana and Hubert, Rascal was leaping straight into the arms of adventure. Freedom was pulling him like a magnet and was as tempting as a mousetrap. The neighbor's rose garden was too hot so they set off for another neighbor's yard. There they practiced creeping up on a sparrow perched on an apple tree. Then they marveled at the robins in flight. The cats craned their necks as they watched the graceful birds soar through the air.

After frolicking with their newfound freedom all afternoon, it came time for a nap. Calls of "it's getting late" and "let's go home" were heard from some cats as the sun began to slowly sink behind the great mountain in the distance. But Rascal advised against it. "Let's sleep now near this spruce tree," he suggested, and they did.

\*\*\*

After an hour Bunny touched Rascal's head. "Let's go home. I'm hungry."

"Hungry, hungry, hungry." Lumby was jumping.

"Let's go home," said Snow and Dandy.

"Let's go because it is a shame," said Sofia.

Philosopher said nothing.

Reluctantly, Rascal agreed with the group. He stood up and said, "Let's go!"

Nobody moved.

Rascal said, "Does anyone know where it is... I mean, which direction is our home?"

Each cat looked in a different direction at the same time. Everybody had their own version of the way back home and each one was ready to go in a different direction. The problem was that there were as many directions as there were cats.

The confusion started their tongues wagging, as arguments broke out amongst the agitated and more than a little confused felines. Their bickering grew in volume until it became almost impossible, amidst all the shouting and yelling, to even understand what anyone was saying.

"Quiet!" commanded Rascal. "I will lead you back the shortest way."

The others were silenced, at least for the moment. They looked at Rascal with a mixture of hope and apprehension.

"Ooooo... do you see?" Rascal said. "We will open this gate and pass quietly along the backyard that has the high wooden fence. Then... just... almost... at our home..." and with those words, Rascal came to the gate and opened it. Something was written on the gate but he had no time to read it.

"How nice here," said Snow, inching along slowly with her tail up.

"Quiet. It is a shame walking into somebody's backyard," whispered Sofia.

"Why not? This is the backyard of our neighbor's neighbor. There is nothing wrong with going to visit our neighbor's neighbor."

"I don't understand," said Lumby.

"Shut up!" puffed Bunny. "I smell a very stinging smell of a dog. It's better if we..."

Bunny never had a chance to finish his sentence. Two huge, drooling Rottweilers emerged directly and Rascal's loud scream pierced the air. "Run for your life! Run!" he shouted and ran with big jumps. The dogs, with their mouths open and sharp fangs bared, were close on his tail.

"Chase the cats! Don't let them get away!"

barked the first dog.

"Chase the thief!" snarled the second dog.

"I have him, I have him, I have him... I almost had him! No, I don't have him. They escaped! For the Cat's Bone!" shouted the first dog angrily.

In the face of danger the cats ran very fast. They stopped behind the fence, all of them thankful to still be in one piece. Tired and frightened, they sat down, surprised because instead of a green hedge and a small white house they saw in front of them a big garbage can that smelled of fish, green salad, and carrots. Next to it someone had tossed an old couch and a worn overcoat with holes.

Rascal said, "Let's go hide in those bushes, then wait until the moon rises. I have a feeling that it will be easier to find our way home, because I remember very well the moon looking into our window. By the way, those dogs will go to sleep."

The tired cats nodded, too exhausted to argue about Rascal's plan. But Philosopher asked quietly, "My orange brother, do you know what was written on the gate?"

"Gee! I didn't want to lose time reading."

"It said: *Beware of angry dogs!*"

"And Grandma calico told us..." Rascal wanted to change the subject. "...she told us about gardens, garbage and streets where friendly cats lived."

"But we did not see even one cat," said Lumby.

"Maybe it was a long time ago and not true," said Dandy.

"True, true, Grandma always says the truth," said Rascal nodding, and quickly added, "but this was the time when there were fewer dogs and more cats."

"It was good for the cats," sighed Dandy.

Philosopher added, "They did what they wanted to do, they went where they wanted to go."

"And they ate when they wanted to eat," said Lumby.

"And slept when and where they wanted to sleep," added Sofia.

"Today life is different," said some strange voice from the right corner of the garbage can.

The group of cats was startled. None of them dared to say a word. Finally, Rascal cleared his throat and said, "Who are you?"

After a short silence, a gray-striped cat came slowly into view. "My name is Stripe," the stranger said. "Do you know how to open the cat's can?"

"Yes! We know that!" said Rascal and Philosopher together.

"For the one hundred thousand mice and one rat!" shouted Stripe. "If I would not be shamed to tears I would tell you how many nights have passed since the last time I ate. And it was only a thin, tiny mouse with more bones than meat. But those cans have been lying around here for a few days. I think somebody forgot them or lost them."

Philosopher was sitting like always with his right ear to the front and his left ear to the back, thinking. Then when his left ear moved to the front and his right ear to the back, he asked, "Is it true?"

"Dreadful to think about," whispered Rascal.

"Ah," sighed Bunny.

"Gee!" Lumby and Snow said at the same time, as they stared with astonishment and compassion.

"Oh, yes!" whispered the gray cat. "Last night – looking tenderly into the rising moon – I rendered homage to the pleasant recollection of those days when I had a can of cat food for the last time."

Bunny brought a stick, Rascal put it into the small eye on the can, and Philosopher started pushing on one side of the stick. There was a cracking sound and slowly the metal lid opened, releasing a tasty smell.

"I love chicken with sauce and green peas and rice," said Stripe happily as he began to devour the food.

"Poor cat, he is so hungry," Snow said with empathy, wanting to lick his head.

\*\*\*

After the third can Stripe slowed down and began to wash his coat, starting with his nose, and moving on to his paws.

The cats watched in silence. They had never witnessed hunger before. All of them were thinking the same thing. How awful it must be for cats like Stripe, never knowing where his next meal might come from. They began to ache for the warm, comfortable home they had so carelessly left behind.

"There is a scarcity of mice?" Rascal asked, breaking into their thoughts.

"This is a very lean year for mice and even rats." Stripe glanced up sadly, and quickly said, "But I have an outstandingly good appetite, which is a sign of good health. People exaggerate a lot and when a cat catches lots of mice, people gossip and say we are greedy. But, if not for our help, people would be destroyed, because mice would eat people."

"Is it true?" asked Philosopher, looking with surprise at the newcomer.

"Oh? Really?" said Rascal.

"Yes, that's right!" the gray cat said, nodding gravely. "True contribution is never recognized."

"And how was it a long time ago? Lots of mice?" asked Sofia, curiously, because she too liked to hunt.

"A lot of mice."

"Ha! And were there rats, too?" asked Snow.

"Even more rats than mice."

"Holy Cat!" groaned Philosopher. "And those fatty moles?"

"And even more moles than mice and rats together!"

"Oh! Oh! And lots of birds?"

"There one hundred times more birds than rats, moles and mice."

"Don't say any more. My whiskers are trembling and my head is dizzy just trying to imagine that much prey."

"What about salmon in the rivers?"

"The rivers were so full of salmon that the water overflowed and burst its banks," Stripe said, his eyes glittering as he told the story.

"Let's dance with joy in that beautiful memory," exclaimed Lumby, performing a somersault.

All the cats started dance of joy, dance of hunting mice, fishing salmon, and opening a cat's can. Philosopher and Rascal opened the rest of the cans, but only those with a loop. They opened so easily, like a can of Coca-Cola. The feast began.

***

The cats ate slowly, occasionally stopping to lick their whiskers, until everyone was full. As they sat back and let the food digest in their stomachs, Stripe told the story of his grandfather hunting forest and field mice with their Grandma calico. His new friends were mesmerized by his fascinating tales of yesteryear.

Suddenly the eyes of two cats peeped from behind the trunk of a huge tree. It was Shaggy, with long orange hair, and Spotted, with short white and black hair. They joined Rascal and the others, and after some small talk they sat and ate from the open cans, meowing with delight.

The moonlit sky was bright and clear. Everything was shimmering in silver and gold. The trees had silver leaves, the grass glittered as if it was sprinkled with silver particles, the garbage can shimmered and even the cats' fur took on a silver glow. With the cans opened, Philosopher, Rascal and the newcomers ate heartily. Silver salmon, chicken, and silver beef with rice and carrots. It was like some sort of a holiday feast. Even humans probably didn't eat this well!

"I have not eaten for a long time," sighed Spotty.

"Those cans were waiting for a long time in the bushes behind the garbage and not one of us wild cats could open them," said Shaggy.

"One hundred thanks!" meowed the wild cats. "You have proven yourselves our friends."

They danced again the dance of joy, the dance of friendship and the dance of the open can.

Sofia touched Rascal gently with her paw. "Let's go home, it is a shame for well behaved cats to be walking at night over garbage cans."

Their celebration came to a sudden halt as Stripe ordered silence. "Now quiet! Do you hear something? It may be my imagination, but I think somebody is creeping up on us. Let's hide, don't trust anyone," he meowed in warning.

The cats dashed for safety, and soon lay hidden under the silver leaves of the horse chestnut tree, staring diligently, straining their ears. All of them could now confirm that Stripe was right after all. Someone was indeed approaching, slowly and cautiously.

"Who are you?" asked Rascal, as always very curious and quick to make the first move.

A loud metallic sound rang out into the night.

"Get out, this is my kingdom."

In the moon's glow, they could see the huge head of a Siamese cat. To say the least, he did not look happy.

"Oh boy, it's Nasty!" whispered Stripe.

"I prohibit dancing and I prohibit opening cans. The patent of opening cans belongs to me." The big cat grimly looked at Philosopher and scornfully snorted to Bunny. "And you without the tail, do you know what the biggest adornment of a cat is?"

Bunny sat and gently answered, "It is his mind."

"You are stupid!" snarled Nasty. "The adornment of a cat is his tail! I see why you have no mind because you have no tail!"

"Did somebody cut off your tail by closing a door on it? Ha, ha, ha, ha," said a tiny voice from behind Nasty.

Nasty turned toward the skinny cat that stood behind him. "This is my helper Clumsy. Maybe he will be a smart cat someday because he has a tail. Even he learned how to bristle his tail in the eye of danger. A cat is nothing without a tail."

No sooner had the mean cat stopped speaking when something terrible snorted and out from the bushes jumped a black cat with yellow eyes. Dread filled everyone except Nasty and his shadow, Clumsy.

"This is Black Claw," Nasty said, introducing his friend as he very proudly pushed his tail up. "Okay, we will make peace! Tomorrow I'm inviting everyone of you to fish for salmon in a small brook that was born in the Rocky Mountains but travels all the way to the Pacific Ocean."

"But what if we get our feet wet?" asked Rascal timidly. He didn't like water and even in the biggest rain he was always dry, because he would run so fast to get out of it.

Nasty glared at Rascal scornfully. "Don't worry, a little wetness is not bad," he said, then quickly added, "Tomorrow your guide will be Clumsy. So until tomorrow's sunrise, I will wait for you by number 5 garbage can, number 3 backyard, number 6 corner and number 10 tree. Look for my scratch marks." He glanced towards Black Claw, who promised to be there at number 10 tree also shortly after the sunrise.

\*\*\*

The wild cats ran off in every direction leaving Rascal and his group alone. After pondering for a long time Rascal decided that after fishing salmon they would go back home. But now it was time to find a comfortable place to sleep for the night. They retreated to a line of trees behind a nearby building and cuddled up as best they could next to one another for warmth and safety. None of them were used to sleeping outside and getting to sleep would have been almost impossible if they hadn't been so tired.

Before going to sleep Sofia asked, "What was the secret you had this morning?"

"Nothing important," murmured Rascal, closing his eyes.

"We were ready to go to our Diana and Hubert to Sedona in Arizona," said Bunny yawning.

"Is it far?"

"Not too far, only 5,000 kilometers, I checked on the map," said Philosopher.

"Are you cats crazy?!" wailed Sofia.

"You're right, it was a stupid idea, but I'm very happy that tomorrow we will sleep in our own beds," said Snow as she snuggled up to Dandy.

"Then why...?" started Lumby, but he did not finish. Although his eyes were open and he heard the cats talking, his mind was already sleeping, dreaming of playing, of dancing... and of home.

\*\*\*

The next day, Nasty came with his gang.

"Okay now, your guide will be Clumsy and you have to listen to him. Every word he says is an order. Meantime I will be on the bottom of the river talking with the fish, so you won't see me. I will tell them to listen to you and be easy to catch. Do you want fish? Yes?"

"There are good and tasty fish in this water?" asked Snow.

Nasty looked at her as if he she said something dumb. He seemed to have no patience for the new group of cats, and his attitude was as if he was doing them a favor that they most certainly did not deserve. "They are much better than the best mouse meat in the world. They have more tender flesh than a fat young mole," he said.

"I have never eaten anything like that ever," said Bunny timidly, ready to jump into the deep water.

Nasty beckoned to Black Claw. They moved to the side and whispered discreetly, knowing that the other cats were watching them intently. With only a few murmurs they understood each other and returned to the cats.

"We are very glad you're here," said Black Claw. "I see that this is the first time you are going to fish for salmon." He seemed more friendly than Nasty.

"Yes!" said Philosopher, nodding, but he soon became lost in thought, his tail swishing lazily.

"I prefer to catch a mouse," said Snow quietly.

"No, no, no," said Black Claw with amusement. "Fishing is much easier. No one will ever believe that you can catch a mouse alive!" He grinned slyly.

Rascal preferred not to go fishing, but didn't want to look like he was afraid of Nasty and his group. So very amiably he said, "Let's go, then! It is pleasure fishing with such a nice company."

"I think it's better to consider what we're doing before jumping into the water," said Philosopher; his right ear took to the front and his left one to the back, his mind deep in thought.

"Why not wait for Stripe? He will be happy too," said Bunny.

"I don't know what he did, but his mother does not allow him to go fishing.  And I purposely did not invite Shaggy because… you don't know him… he would eat all our fish… until the last bone!  He is a glutton." replied Black Claw.

While talking they came to the shore of the small river.  Nasty said, "Now we will find the best place to fish."  He seemed anxious to get things started. He had walked in front of the others the entire way. "Now, get ready, and on the order of Clumsy you guys jump into the river.  Meantime I'm going to put on my invisible attire to dive and talk to the fish, so they will be more willing to be taken by you."  He winked at them and with one jump he slipped away into the bushes to hide.

As the cats climbed up onto the bank of the river, they had mixed feelings.  Some of them were excited at the prospect of doing something that seemed fun and new.  But some of the others were a bit scared by the whole thing.

Clumsy stood in front of the group.  "Very good!" he said.  "Close your eyes and wait for my order.  I will say, 'Now.'  If you open even one eye before you hear my order, you will lose two eyes!  Not only one!"

Bunny bristled with fear as he listened with one ear to Clumsy's voice giving his last minute instructions.  "On my order, one, two, three…"  And with the second ear Bunny caught the tiny happy voice of Lumby.  "Hey, butterfly… chase… go…

I have... oops... he flies too fast..."

Bunny wanted to shout to Lumby not to go too far after the butterfly but the strong voice of Clumsy stopped him. "Four, five, now! Jump!"

\*\*\*

The cats jumped. Rascal hesitated but Black Claw helped him make the decision and pushed him into river. When Rascal touched the wet cold water he screamed so loudly that leaves fell from the trees. Then he shouted, "Get out... fast... it is betrayal!"

Bunny, Sofia, Snow and Dandy did not wait one second. They swam quickly to the shore. There was no sight of Nasty, Black Claw or Clumsy. They all vanished somewhere.

Bunny shook his fur like all wet cats do and started looking for Lumby. "Lumby! Where are you?"

Not noticing any of this, Lumby was happily chasing another butterfly. Sofia was lamenting and crying loudly. Dandy was helping Snow to get rid of water out of her ear. Then they noticed that Rascal and Philosopher were not there. They looked around everywhere, but the two brothers were nowhere to be seen. Sofia cried even more loudly, joined by Snow. "They are dead," they lamented.

Bunny, not wasting any time complaining, spotted something orange on top of a tree. "It's Rascal! He's alive! He's on the tree on the other side of the river!"

"Philosopher is gone! Help him! The river took him down! Help! Help!" shouted Rascal. "Save my brother, please! Save Philosopher!"

Sofia and Snow stopped crying. They noticed Philosopher fighting to stay above the water. "Let's go help our Philosopher," shouted Dandy.

"Let's go," said Lumby joyfully, thinking this was some sort of a game. And with a big smile from one ear to the other, he said, "Yes, I see our Philosopher; he's having lots of fun! I'd like to join him!"

Bunny did not say anything; he only murmured something looking very concerned. He ran along the shore in the direction where Philosopher was being swept down the river, but lost sight of him around a curve. Lumby followed him with joyful jumps.

Suddenly, like an answer to calls for help, from out of the blue came a yellow Labrador. The big dog bounded past Bunny and said, "Don't worry, I will help you guys. I have also had a very bad time with Nasty's gang." Then he disappeared behind the curve.

The stunned cats waited impatiently, pacing back and forth, not knowing what to expect. "We have to do something," Bunny said. "How do we know if we can really trust that dog?"

They began to argue amongst themselves over what they should do. Should they stay put, or run after the dog and try to help Philosopher?

As they were bickering, the Labrador came back with the wet cat, who did not resemble any cat at all.

The dog carried him gently, but firmly in his mouth, the way a mother cat carries her kittens.

Lumby still thought it was a game, but Bunny was beginning to panic. "Oh no, is he dead?" he panted. Their friend Philosopher was not moving, and he didn't make a sound.

\*\*\*

Thankfully, after an extended time of everyone's horror Philosopher began to reawaken. He opened one eye, looked around, and then almost immediately he became energized as his adrenaline kicked in. He shouted, "Where is Rascal? Where is my brother?"

"Rascal! Rascal!" Sofia screeched.

Then Bunny chimed in, "Not long ago I saw him at the other side of the river, up on the big tree."

"Rascal! Rascal!" Sofia and Snow echoed.

The dog was waiting silently, then looked up. Somebody was calling him. It was a human being. "Biscuit! Here, boy... come here, let's go."

From the far shore the cats could hear a meow, "I'm here, come here." It was Rascal!

"No, you come here," they all shouted in unison.

"Let's go," Philosopher said. "He might be hurt." But some of the others were hesitant. Finally, after long deliberation, they decided that they would not go unless they found a bridge. So, they turned around and walked away looking for one...

\*\*\*

Rascal was left all alone as the others went away on the other side of the river. At first, he wanted to wait for his friends to find him, but after a while he decided to find a bridge on his own. He noticed that the other cats went down the river. His logic told him to go the same direction. He was afraid as he walked along, and every time he heard a sound he would jump into the trees to hide.

His imagination was whispering into his ear: *"If you happen to get home alone say that somebody kidnapped you and all the other cats. But you were very smart to escape. They tried to catch you but you jumped, bit them, and..."* He didn't really like the idea of telling lies, but how else could he explain why they were away from the house for so long? Rascal knew that there was no easy answer. All he really wanted now was to find his friends, or for them to find him.

\*\*\*

The other cats felt bad about leaving Rascal alone, but they hoped to find a bridge quickly. Their only desire now was to pick Rascal up and get back home as soon as possible. They dreamed about their white house, flowers in the garden, and the green hedge around it. Why had they ever left? Would they find Rascal on the other side of the river? Would they ever get back home?

It was not an easy task to find a bridge in unfamiliar territory. It was a long and difficult walk. They all became tired and hungry.

"Those cans were very good and tasty," remarked Snow sadly.

"I will give one cat's life for that food," added Dandy.

"Me too... but where is Rascal?" asked Philosopher, dejected.

"Don't worry," said troubled Sofia. She hoped her voice sounded strong and confident, but she knew that it probably did not.

All the way Lumby kept asking, "When will we have supper? How long will it take to get home?" Then he complained about being tired, and about his paws starting to hurt. He had an itch in his left ear and his tail was getting heavy.

Sofia murmured through her teeth: "It is all my fault! My fault! I could have stopped them at home, closed the door, told Tom. It is my fault."

"The bridge! I see the bridge!" suddenly exclaimed Dandy. They all rushed towards it. As they were nearing the bridge, they noticed Rascal climbing up to them from under it. Philosopher leaped upon him and gave him a big cat hug. "Brother! You are alive! I thought I would never see you again." Two tears went down his cheeks, but then he got himself back under control and said: "In any case, brother, it is good to find you safe and sound."

Rascal smiled widely. "Don't make your hair

bristle for my sake, Philosopher," he replied. "I'm fine. Nothing to fear. I still have all of my nine lives."

Everyone was happy to have found Rascal and they all wanted to talk with him, but before they had a chance they heard a meow. It was Mau, an Egyptian cat. He was silver with black speckles and green eyes. He marched from the woods onto the trail in front of them and stopped them in their tracks. "I'm Mau. It means 'cat' in the Egyptian language. Welcome to my kingdom. You look tired and hungry. I invite you for a supper..."

\*\*\*

After the supper of fish, the exhausted group of cats quickly fell asleep. In the morning, while chatting with Mau, Rascal told his new friend that he was a tamed cat.

"You are tamed?" asked Mau curiously. "What does that mean? Tamed?"

"Tamed means to have ties..."

"Please tell me more, clearly."

"For you, every human resembles every other human, and for humans you resemble every other cat."

"How many cats are there?" interrupted Lumby.

"As many as there are stars in the sky," said Rascal.

"How many stars are there?"

"As many as there are cats."

"Okay," said Lumby, nodding as he lay down close to Bunny. He wanted them to think he understood. But actually, the strange answer just made him even more confused. "Maybe tonight I will have to count the stars," he thought. "Then I will know."

Now Rascal could continue with his explanation of what it meant to be tamed. "When you get tamed, each one of you will be needed. You will be the most important cat in the whole world, and this person who tamed you will be the most important one for you in the entire world! You will be the best, the most loved cat on the planet. If some child tames you, you will hear and recognize his or her steps from afar, and you will easily know the difference between their steps and those of other people. On the sound of strangers you will not react."

"How can I do that?" asked Mau.

"You have to be very patient. In the beginning you will sit not too far from the gate of a garden that you like and choose. Just sit, and observe the house. Don't say anything even if someone tries to talk to you. But every day come closer and closer. After five days you may accept some food. Then... then..." stammered Rascal, "be happy when they touch you... and PURR. The more you purr the wider their heart will open for you."

He paused for a while, and then continued: "I will tell you a secret – it is better to see with the heart, instead of eyes. The eyes are blind. Don't choose people based on the look of their clothing or the color of their skin because your eyes are blind; you should look with your heart. There is something more – the decision to be tamed brings about tears..."

"We need to get going" interrupted Sofia. "There is a long way ahead of us."

*** 

Mau became thoughtful and depressed when it was time to say good-bye to his new friends. "I am sorry you have to leave; I feel bonded with you after this short encounter"

"Don't worry, our ties are like tiny, invisible threads, and one day those threads will pull us together."

"Who knows, who knows," said Philosopher to himself and smiled.

The cats walked quietly away, and after some time Rascal noticed, "It looks like today we will eat supper at home."

"Are we going in the right direction?" asked Sofia, furrowing her nose.

"Wait a minute, wait a minute," murmured Rascal, scratching his ear.

Philosopher became stressed, as he could read the tone of his brother's voice, and he knew that something was not right. "We'll ask the first cat that we meet," said Rascal. "He should be able to help us find our way home."

"Do you remember Grandma's secret solution to lost things?" asked Dandy. "They are not really lost, only misplaced somewhere. Here is what you need to do if you lose something: first you need to quietly sit down and step-by-step think back what you had been doing with that thing before you lost it..."

"What is the conclusion for us?" interrupted Sofia. "We cannot trace our steps back home!"

As the others discussed the best plan to get home, Bunny sat busily studying the sky. "Looks like a storm is coming," he said, his voice starting to tremble.

"Let's go faster," urged Snow. "The storm is coming."

"Yes, it is very dangerous," lamented Sofia, looking warily at the coming clouds.

"Look, there are two cats coming!" shouted Snow.

"Let's ask them where we are," decided Dandy, running towards them.

Philosopher murmured to himself, "One of them looks like our Grandma after a trip into the factory chimney – calico, but dirty with soot. Another one is pale orange as if he had anemia."

Rascal ran ahead of the others and said, "Good morning. Excuse me, I have a little question to ask you. Where are we?"

"This same place where we are," answered the 'sooted' calico with a broad smile.

"Where are you, then?"

"Opposite yourselves."

Rascal didn't like the way this was going. Were they just kidding, or were these cats really going to give them a hard time instead of helping them? Rascal tried his best to be diplomatic. "I know you are very funny and good in playing the word games. I would enjoy that in other circumstances, but we need to find our garbage can and our home. It is not too far from the wooden fence and the backyard with two Rottweilers. Are you able to help us?"

"In that case, come with us," said the older of the two cats, the dirty looking one.

"Where are you going?"

"For us it doesn't matter, we are just going ahead."

Then the cats introduced themselves. The pale orange cat was named Marmalade and the dirty one was called What-What.

\*\*\*

As it turned out, the two cats were very talkative and friendly. They knew the neighborhood and they even knew whether to expect rain or a storm just by observing the dancing mosquitoes. They said that they speak four languages, and that they knew how deep moles dig. They could also name all the flowers in the forest and each of the stars in the sky. They knew the number of wild geese coming for the winter to the Cat-opolis-Metropolis.

What-What added, "Those sparrows without a tail... I'm proud to say, that was our work."

And Marmalade said, "We always smile, even when it rains, because we still remember the sun. When everyone is hot with the sun, we still feel the fresh rain and we smile, remembering yesterday's nice rain."

The group walked along beside their two new friends for over an hour. Finally they came to a familiar garbage can that smelled of fish, green salad, carrots, an old couch, and a worn overcoat with holes.

Sofia started planning what she would do when she gets home. She was going to make a big wash and clean her fur. Snow was thinking about sleeping in a nice soft bed. And Lumby planned nothing, but started to dance a dance of a happy return to the garbage can. Rascal, Philosopher, Bunny and Dandy were disputing about politics in the country and across the borders.

Bunny said, "The president of Catland should be a Japanese Bobtail." That surprised no one, because Japanese bobtails were quite similar to Bunny. "Those cats are very active, intelligent and very talkative. Their soft voices are capable of nearly a whole scale of tunes, like singing. Besides, those cats like to travel, they do not panic in a hotel room, and they adjust to dogs and other animals. They have very unique tails. But more importantly, the Japanese Bobtail brings good luck in business. For that reason you see them everywhere in shops, restaurants, and offices." He was right about that. Just about everyone has seen them somewhere in statue form, a porcelain cat with a raised paw.

What-What favored Korat, the cat from Thailand. "They have extraordinary powers of hearing, sight and scent," he shouted happily and added, "so this president will hear, will see, and will smell everything that happens inside the country and beyond its borders. Besides, Korat is a symbol of good fortune and a silver cat means wealth. Korat never changes color, and his fur and hair are the same silver-blue from his first day of life until he dies."

"But I've heard that his eyes change with age," said Bunny.

"That is true."

"Would that be good or bad for a president?" asked Bunny.

"How is it with Korat's eyes?" asked Snow, curiously. She couldn't help listening to what the guys were talking about.

"The eyes of Korat are like those of no other cat, with an expressive and intense gaze. It is not possible to lie to them or to trick them into making a bad choice. Imagine, my dears, how it would be to have a president to whom nobody could lie!" said What-What.

"What color are Korat's eyes?" asked Sofia, because sometimes she liked to talk about politics too.

"Like with all newborn kittens, at first their

eyes are blue, changing to amber with a green tinge around the pupil during adolescence. After 2 to 4 years of age, the eyes are luminous green. Oh, I almost forgot, their hair does not float off when they are being stroked and petted, so it is very good for allergic people. Even someone with allergies can pet and care for such president."

Now Sofia asked about the color of a Korat's fur.

"The roots of Korat's hair are light bluish, darkening father, before the ends become silver-tipped. The silvering over the whole body makes a halo, or aura, effect and the close-lying fur shines like a polished silver dollar."

\*\*\*

The cats could talk about politics all night but suddenly Rascal noticed that Lumby was missing. Bunny jumped up and ran behind the garbage can. There was the kitten, eating fresh ground beef from inside a metal box.

"What are you doing?" shouted Bunny.

And Sofia, horrified, said, "It is a shame to eat from somebody's plate."

The cats came closer and, indeed, there was lots of fresh ground beef on a plate.

"Dinner arrived by itself," said Lumby, happily.

Marmalade looked terrified, and Rascal scolded, "It could be poisonous meat from Nasty!"

Philosopher checked it carefully, smelled it, and

sat down to think. Then he said, "No smell of Nasty, only some people."

When Marmalade heard the word "people," all hair on his tail stood straight up. "Uh-oh," he said. "I think that means it is time for me to say good-bye." He explained that he was afraid of people. What-What agreed, saying that they only liked organic rats, mice, moles, and sometimes birds.

\*\*\*

The metal box was big enough and comfortable. Everybody decided to join Lumby in the feast. They ate in silence, their new friends having departed. Suddenly they heard big noise and they found themselves in pitch darkness...

"The storm is coming! Run! Run fast home!" several of the cats shouted simultaneously. But they could not run as it was not possible to see anything.

"What is this?" they asked each other as the box began shaking.

"I don't know, it looks like the wind is coming. Better sit in this sheltered place and wait until the storm is over," Philosopher advised.

"I'm afraid of thunderstorms and lightning," whispered Sofia, crying.

"Why are you so frightened?" Philosopher asked compassionately. "It is just a part of nature."

Sofia told them the story of a long time ago in her country when she was small. A thunderbolt hit very close and she was hidden under the bed for 3 days without food and water.

"Geeee! Three days!" meowed Rascal. "I know about one brown cat who went two weeks without water and food."

"How is it possible?" asked Philosopher. "I would be dead after five hours of starvation."

"Yes, it is possible. The cat was closed inside a container, and when the ship came to America seamen found the cat after two weeks' journey."

"Alive?" asked Snow, surprised.

"Yes, alive, but very thin. It was his good luck that he had nine lives before he boarded that ship."

\*\*\*

Instead of fleeing, the frightened cats stayed put until the storm passed by them. After some time everything became quiet and the darkness was gone; but instead of green leaves of the tree they saw a cement ceiling, big boots, pants, two arms and a head in a hat. A pair of strange hands reached down and caught Lumby. The terrified kitten stared at the man, who glared back at him and then dropped him onto the ground. They found themselves in some sort of enclosed pen, and they could see no way out.

"I have you, thieves! Every night you steal meat, chickens, and rabbits from my house. Now you will pay with your furs."

Rascal looked like he was sorry for all that had

happened, and Sofia was ready to take all the blame, even if somebody had stolen a horse, a cow and 40 sheep.

The Stranger went out and Bunny asked, "Lumby, are you okay?"

"Meow," the kitten happily answered, "we have lots of fun, don't we?"

Philosopher sat on his tail and thought about what he had heard. Rascal turned fast around, hitting something with his head so hard, he saw stars. Sofia was wringing her paws, Snow was crying. Dandy, choking on his own saliva complained, "We get sentenced to death and he is laughing!"

Sofia was asking for a miracle. Philosopher was sitting with two ears turned to the front, which meant that he was in deep meditation. Then he said, "I remember when our Grandma told us, 'Never lose your courage even in the face of black clouds around you. Think and use all your ideas, even those ideas that may appear as though they would not work. Do not sit and wait for a miracle. The hidden energy of hope, together with action, will attract help from a new, unexpected direction. Crying, fear, and anger do not help at all.'"

Rascal's head cleared from the last star and he began to think of ways to escape. Lumby was hunting for spiders, flies, and moths, kicking up the dust. Bunny was thinking about ways of escaping. Sofia switched from praying to weeping, and she said between sneezes and tears, "Here we will die, we will all die."

"If only we could die quickly instead of enduring terrible suffering before we die," hoped Snow.

"Do not cry," whispered Bunny. Then he went to check the walls.

*\*\*\**

It was getting dark and they anticipated the longest night of their lives. Bunny did not give up, and he found a place where it was possible to dig under the wall. He began furiously scratching his claws into the hard, brown dirt...

Lumby, playful as usual, suddenly shouted, "Flying mouse!" He jumped on a pile of bottles making a lot of noise.

"Hey, what's that?" came the voice of the Stranger.

They all hid. But they heard nothing. He must have gone away again.

When they all emerged from their hiding places, Lumby asked how it was possible for a mouse to fly. Bunny, tired from digging, patiently explained that it was not a flying mouse but a bat. Lumby had never heard of a bat before. To him, it was still a flying mouse.

Bunny went back to digging. After some more time the hole was ready. Now the cats waited into the night for the Stranger to go to sleep.

As the sun went down, things were growing tense as the group of felines got ready to make their move.

"I think somebody is watching us. I feel their eyes on me," said Bunny.

Lumby announced that he saw a ghost, a mouse ghost.

No one believed him, but Lumby insisted that he'd seen the white ghost-mouse sitting on the saddle at the wall. They all decided that the playful kitten was just making up stories again.

*** 

As darkness continued to gather, the cats began to put their plan into action. One by one they went through the hole just to find another room with walls and ceiling. Rascal spotted a door and managed to open it. It was the Stranger's room that smelled of alcohol and cigars. The man was sleeping on the armchair, snoring loudly.

Rascal was looking for another escape route, but the door would not open. The windows were dirty and covered with spider webs. They hid under a table on the far side of the room.

After a while Lumby had enough of this strange play as he was hungry. He ran towards the Stranger before Bunny could stop him. He climbed onto the man's lap and started purring and kneading with his paws like he used to do at home.

The other cats held their breath. Sofia almost fainted. Lumby wanted cat food and he knew that this often worked.

What the cats didn't know, what the Stranger didn't know, and what Lumby did not understand, was that the purring of a cat has a lot of power, like unconditional love. It is not known why cats purr, but it has been established that cats' purring helps people reduce stress.

Lumby warmed the cold heart of the Stranger. He opened his eyes, smiled gently and took the kitten in his arms. He looked at him for a long time. After what seemed like a thousand years, the man stood up and went to the table, poured milk into his plate and let the kitten drink. "You're such a cute little thing," the Stranger said, petting Lumby affectionately. He started talking to the kitten, telling him with slurred words that nobody understood how sad and lonely he was. Lumby licked the man's face and the man smiled.

"That's one dead cat!" swore a tiny voice from somewhere under the table.

Rascal understood that someone from outside their own group was also hidden there. The cats looked around and saw nothing.

"Who are you?" whispered Rascal.

"It's me," came a voice from nowhere. "Promise not to harm me."

The cats nodded. They realized that it was a mouse.

"Please swear on your nine lives."

"Yes, we swear."

"Never in my life have I seen a white mouse,"

remarked Dandy.

"Well, now you have," replied the white mouse. "And I am here to warn you. If you don't do something right now, you will never get your little kitten back."

Philosopher seemed confused. From their hiding place under the table Lumby seemed perfectly safe, joyfully playing with the man. "I don't understand," Philosopher said. "He doesn't seem to be in any danger."

"We should never trust a mouse," whispered Sofia, eyeing the small creature suspiciously.

"I am telling you the truth," declared the white mouse. "My family and I have lived in mouse holes in this man's house for many years. He is a bitter and angry man. His wife and son left him because he loved his alcohol more than he loved them. Now he hates all people and all animals. He has tried to kill me and my family many times. Thankfully, he was too drunk to set his mouse traps right, and he never got us. But he has come close to it."

Rascal now joined in the conversation. "But look how gentle he is with Lumby. I don't think he will hurt him."

The white mouse thought about it for a moment. "Maybe not," he said. "He does seem to like the little fellow. But that, too, will be a problem. For now he will never let him go. He will take him as his own pet, and you will never see him again."

Rascal arched his back. "We shall see about

that!" he said angrily.

"Now, Rascal, don't do anything foolish," Bunny warned.

Not backing down, Rascal said, "But we can't just sit here and do nothing. We're not going home without Lumby."

As the cats bickered, the white mouse sprang into action. He scampered across the floor, his tiny paws making a scratching sound as he went.

"What is that noise?" asked the Stranger, still holding Lumby as he pulled up the table-cloth to look underneath the table. The table-cloth was dirty and old, and had a picture of Santa Claus even though it was summer.

"Must just be my imagination," the Stranger said, starting to play with the kitten again.

The white mouse dashed toward the tall man and ran straight up the inside of his pants leg! The man began jumping around as he tried in vain to understand what was happening to him. He dropped Lumby to the floor. Rascal ran out of his hiding place, grabbed the confused kitten, and pulled him away. "Come with me!" he shouted.

"Where are we going, Rascal? I was having fun," Lumby protested.

"We're going home, little one. We're going home."

They reached their friends just as the Stranger staggered to the door. He opened it and ran outside, screaming. He left the door open, so the cats seized upon the opportunity and scrambled out the door to the freedom of the outside world.

The Stranger was shaking his legs fiercely until finally they saw the white mouse pop out. The man cursed at him as the mouse dashed into the safety of nearby bushes. The man shook his head, pumped his fist and said, "I'll get you one of these days, mouse! Mark my words; I'm going to get you!" He took one more look around and returned to the building, slamming the door behind him.

*** 

The cats cautiously made their way over to the bushes. Philosopher whispered, "Are you in there, my little friend? Are you OK?"

Waltzing out of the bushes as if nothing out of the ordinary had happened, the white mouse said, "Of course I am OK."

The cats thanked him for his help. "You showed tremendous courage," said Rascal."

"For a mouse," added Sofia.

Smiling, the white mouse said, "Maybe someday you can come back here and reward me with some cheese. But for now, I think you'd better get going. I'm sure you have people back home who are worried sick over you."

They all agreed that he was right. And it made them feel warm inside (and a bit guilty) when they realized that Tom must be looking everywhere for them.

"Thank you," shouted the cats and said a friendly good bye. Then they were on their way again.

\*\*\*

As they were again getting tired from long walking, they noticed a huge building in the distance. Their eyes widened. "What is that place?" Lumby asked.

"I believe it is called a supermarket," said Philosopher. "It is a place where humans get their food."

The other cats were confused.

"Like a trash barrel?" asked Dandy.

"Or a tin can with a lid?" asked Sofia.

"No, this is different," Philosopher said. "This is a place where they…well, it's hard to explain."

"Maybe the best way to explain it is for us to go take a look ourselves," Rascal suggested.

The others all thought that was a great idea. Though tired, they somehow mustered up the energy to run the rest of the way. Soon they found themselves in an enormous parking lot. Cars were everywhere.

"Be careful now," Bunny cautioned. "We don't want anyone to get run over."

It was kind of scary for all of them, having so many cars that close by. Lumby, of course, didn't seem to mind. He was playing a dangerous game of weaving in and out of the fast moving traffic. Rascal ran up to the youth and pulled him out of the way. He thought about giving a safety lecture to the little guy, but then he remembered how he used to behave back when he was that age, so he just smiled at the memory and the group followed some people into the store.

They were shocked when the doors opened automatically as people stepped in front of them. The cats stealthily walked down one of the long, brightly lit aisles. Their noses were twitching at all of the exotic smells.

"Never in my life have I seen this much food," Philosopher exclaimed in astonishment.

"They have fish, and meat, all kinds of sweet stuff...It's like Cat Heaven," said an extremely excited Dandy.

Just as they were really starting to get into their exploration of this remarkable place, something terrible happened. Before any of them had a chance to run, a big net came down on top of them, trapping the entire group.

"Ah-ha, now I've got you," they heard someone say. They felt themselves being lifted up as somebody, a man wearing some sort of smock, like he must have worked at the store, scooped them up in the net and carried them into a storage room in the back. He dumped them out of the net and left them in a closet. They then heard the man close the door and lock it.

*** 

"We're trapped!" screeched Bunny. "How are we ever going to get out?"

There was a dim light on in the closet. They could all see the anger on Sofia's face. "This is all your fault, Rascal!" she shouted. "If we had not followed you we would never have gotten into this horrid situation in the first place."

The others began to murmur amongst themselves, agreeing with Sofia that she was right, that this was indeed all Rascal's fault.

Rascal curled up in a corner, feeling guilty.

"Now wait just a minute," Philosopher said, trying to assess the situation fairly. "None of us were forced to follow my brother. We did it on our own free will. We all know the old saying that 'Curiosity killed the cat.' Well, my friends, we were all curious. Yes, Rascal may have been our leader. But we – each one of us – were all too willing to be his followers."

The group knew he was right. They gathered around Rascal and apologized and tried to bring his spirits back up. But they were all still very frightened. And very sad.

Footsteps approached.

"Oh no!" shouted Bunny. "We're doomed!"

Rascal stepped forward. "I will leap out at whoever opens the door," he said. "Then as I scratch him the rest of you can make a dash for your freedom."

Lumby cuddled up to him and said, "No Rascal. We won't leave you behind."

"The little one is right, my brother," Philosopher said. "Whatever happens to us, we will all face it together."

Just then, the door opened. The cats, all grouped together now, could not believe their eyes.

"Tom!" Lumby yelled with joy. It was incredible that he was here. The kitten jumped up into the boy's arms and began licking him uncontrollably.

Tom smiled broadly. "I'm so happy to see you guys," he said. "I thought I might never see you again. Diana and Hubert have been worried sick about you. They even talked their parents into coming home early from their trip to Arizona."

He turned to the man with the smock and handed him a $20 bill. "Here is your reward, sir," he said. "Thank you so much for finding my cats."

The man popped the money into his pocket. "My pleasure, son," he said in a gruff voice. "If they ever get lost again, just put up another one of those reward posters in my store and I'll be happy to find them again for you."

"Thanks, but no thanks," said Tom, smiling. "I'm not letting these guys out of my sight ever again."

# EPILOGUE

Three days had passed since the cats had returned home. Their reunion with Diana and Hubert was a joyous occasion. Now they were once again back in their old, familiar attic, and back to their old habits. Rascal was curled up in his favorite spot, in the third drawer of the old cabinet. He had his diary out, and a lot of writing to catch up on.

*Dear Diary:*

*It's me, Rascal, again. I've been away from home for a few days. We all went on an adventure. Wow, I never knew the world outside of the house was so big! It gets scary sometimes (well...I was never scared, of course, but I know some of the others were) but we had a lot of fun too.*

*Still, it's so good to be back home again. I now know why we have rules: for our own good. There's a lot of trouble a cat can get into if he's not careful.*

*Now, don't get me wrong, dear diary, I'm not saying I won't ever leave the house again. I'm still curious about those big mountains I can see from out this very window. What is over there? What does it look like? What does it feel like to look down on everything from the top of the world? Someday my curiosity will make me go to find out...*

*But for now, just enjoying life here with my friends is good enough for me. This adventure taught me what true friendship is really all about. I now realize that...*

As Rascal was writing, he was interrupted by the sound of the family car pulling up into the driveway outside. Lumby jumped up. "They just got back from the supermarket!" he said excitedly.

Rascal remembered that magical place. And all the great food that came from there. He leapt up onto the windowsill and saw Diana and Hubert and their parents taking shopping bags out from the back of their van.

He dashed back to his perch in the third drawer of the cabinet. He continued:

*Tomorrow is another day and I am sure there are new adventures to come. But right now it's chow time, they're sure to have brought home plenty of good stuff. And sometimes, these simple pleasures are more than enough, even for a rascal of a cat like me.*

# Part 2

# Enchanted Forest

Rascal, the cat, was curled up in his favorite spot in a drawer in an old cabinet in the attic. It was a hot summer day, and the heat in the attic made the air feel thick and heavy. It was dark except for a shaft of sunlight that pierced the window several feet above Rascal's head. Dust motes danced in its brightness. The mischievous cat was doing what he enjoyed most – writing his diary.

*Though it was months ago, I can't stop thinking about that great adventure we had. Yes, what a big world there is outside of this house! I saw just a tiny part of it. The world is so huge! I felt like a flea on the back of a mouse. I want to see more! I want...*

"Scribbling away again in that diary of yours, my brother?"

Rascal put down his pen and looked up. It was his brother, Philosopher. He did not look or act like Rascal at all; he had a white spot on his nose and he was very slow.

"What brings you here?" Rascal said, eyeing his brother suspiciously. "Why aren't you with all the others in the basement, where it is cool?"

Philosopher stretched out all four paws and casually padded over to his brother. "Because it's getting too crowded down there," he said. "I need some space to do my thinking."

Ah yes, thinking. That was all that ever seemed to matter to Philosopher. It always baffled Rascal why his brother could not just enjoy life. He always had to try to figure things out.

"Maybe you do too much thinking," Rascal said.

Philosopher didn't seem amused. "And maybe you do too much writing," he said.

Rascal arched his back. "Ha! There is no such thing as too much writing. If it were not for writers, you would not have all those books you read."

The wise thinker cat thought about that for a moment. "You make a good point, my brother. But what is it you are writing in that diary anyway? Let me see," he said and made a move to take the diary.

"No!" shouted Rascal. "It is private."

"Private? Why would you want to keep secrets from your brother?"

"Just because..."

Philosopher shook his head. "Oh, I understand. You must be embarrassed by what you are writing. I am sure it is something quite foolish," he said and began to walk away.

"Foolish? Ha! If only you knew, my brother. I am writing a great story. It came to me in a dream."

Now, the truth of the matter is, Rascal was telling his brother a fib. The "great story" was really just his descriptions of the everyday life of an everyday cat. But he couldn't let Philosopher know that! His brother always thought he was so smart. Rascal wanted to do something that smarty pants could not do. Writing a great story was the first thing that came to mind.

Philosopher peered at his brother. "Great fishbone, Rascal," he said, "then why keep it to yourself? Why not share your story with all of us?"

Rascal had to think quickly. He said, "Because it is not finished. But just wait, tonight, after Diana and Hubert have gone to bed, I will meet all of you right here. And I will read my story to you. All of you will be amazed!"

Diana and Hubert were sister and brother – the cats' beloved owners. Though just young children, they seemed big to the cats, and all of them loved to gain their attention and respect.

"Amazed?" said Philosopher skeptically. "We shall see. I am going to tell the others now. But I will return… and we will see how great your story really is."

With that, Philosopher leaped onto the stairs and scampered away.

Rascal was left alone with his thoughts. He thought. And he thought. And he thought some more. He began scribbling down some ideas. Then he erased what he wrote. He wrote some more, looked at it… then erased it again. "This is just no good," he shouted in frustration, and threw his diary onto the floor beneath his cozy drawer in the cabinet. He sat in silence for who knows how long. Then he decided to take a cat nap…

\*\*\*

"Wake up, Rascal.  Wake up!"

It was Lumby, a playful little white and black kitten with long hair and two black hearts on the back of his white feet.  The youngest of the cats, he was dancing joyfully in front of Rascal.

Rascal rubbed the sleep off his eyes and looked at the clock at the wall.  It was 9:09, cats' favorite time that reminded them – twice a day – of their nine lives.

Looking to his left and to his right, Rascal noticed that all of the other cats in the house had gathered around him.

Sofia, a very sophisticated cat who had moved here from Poland, said, "Diana and Hubert have gone to bed, and we are here to listen to your great story, just as Philosopher told us."

Philosopher gave his brother Rascal a grin that looked like the cat that had swallowed the canary.

"Yes," Philosopher said.  "We are all here, ready for your story.  It's all right there in that diary of yours, is it not?"

Rascal looked at his diary down on the floor.  He leaped down from the cabinet and retrieved it.  Then he quickly returned to his drawer, the one spot where he felt the safest.  "That's right, it is all in there," he lied, knowing he fell asleep without writing a single word.  "But I have the whole story in my memory," he said, "so I can tell you the story without even opening one page."

"That's awesome," Lumby said enthusiastically, launching into his dance of joy. "Tell us! Tell us!"

Rascal could see that the others were getting anxious too. And impatient. So he cleared his throat and began...

This story came to me a in a dream. It is about a time long, long ago, in the faraway place where our ancestors came from. The cats who came before us were like us in many ways. In fact, they even had the same names that we have today. Each one of us is named after each one of them. They lived in a pleasant valley between the two great mountain peaks. Just beyond the valley, however, to the east, was a mysterious place called the Enchanted Forest. There were many stories of cats that wandered into this forbidden place and never came back...

\*\*\*

One day, a cat named Rascal was out and about looking for something to do. He was a curious cat, and always hoped to find something new and different each and every day. On that day, though he was warned not to, he made his way to the Enchanted Forest. As he walked down a certain path, out of the corner of his eye he spied somebody following him. Rascal dashed behind a tree and waited. Then he spotted a tiny white mouse creeping down the path looking nervously in all directions. Rascal leaped down out of the tree and grabbed the mouse in his paws. His mouth watered as he prepared to enjoy the unexpected snack.

Just as he opened his mouth, the frightened mouse cried out, "Please, sir, do not eat me! Please let me tell you my story!"

For some reason, Rascal had pity on the little mouse and put her down. "Go on," he said. "I like to hear good stories."

The little mouse, whose name was Ala, explained that she was two months old and she was looking for her mother, Bala, and two sisters, Cala and Dala. They had been kidnapped and made into servants by a Prehistoric Mouse who lived in the Enchanted Forest. The Prehistoric Mouse, named Tram-bam-bu, was huge and bad and wanted to change everyone to look like a mouse, eat like a mouse and even smell like a mouse. She had long hair, even on her tail, which was the color of a grizzly bear. Her daughter, Tumbaramba, was pink with some blond hair, and her son, Pamparamba, was blue with dark hair. Their father, Tatataramba, was the color of a grizzly but with more black hair. He was away on a trip to the Arctic to meet with the Arctic mice, Ala explained. Rascal had never even heard of the Arctic.

"Why should I help a mouse," Rascal asked.

"Because," the mouse said, "Tram-bam-bu will not be satisfied just when she controls all the mice. She then wants to make all of the animals like mice, and then the mice will rule the planet!"

Rascal said, "I don't know why, but for some reason I believe you. I will not allow that to happen. If any animal is going to rule the Earth, it will be cats! Now, go away and hide. I will come back here tomorrow with my friends. No mouse, not even a Prehistoric one, is going to scare us away."

\*\*\*

The next day Rascal and his friends came to the edge of the Enchanted Forest. Sofia was afraid to go into the Enchanted Forest so they rested in the meadow at the entrance. "This is crazy, Rascal," she said. "We should not help that mouse. It is some kind of mouse trick, I tell you. Everyone knows mice are really just little rats."

As the two of them argued, Lumby, the young kitten, was playing around and disappeared. Bunny, a one-year-old white and gray without a tail, went looking for him, and the others followed. Even Sofia, who usually was reluctant to do such things. They couldn't find Lumby but they came across his tracks leading directly into the Enchanted Forest. There was nothing left to do but to follow the tracks, even into this forbidden and mysterious place they all feared.

***

About a mile into the Enchanted Forest, Rascal got separated from the others when he stopped to smell some flowers. Suddenly, right in his way, stood a strange huge animal. It was a Prehistoric Cat named Samuel. Samuel's white fur was long with black dots. "Yikes! You're the biggest cat I've ever seen," said Rascal.

"That's because you've never seen a Prehistoric Cat," Samuel said. "Why are you here in the Enchanted Forest?"

Rascal explained his encounter with Ala, the tiny white mouse, and how he wanted to help her.

"Well," said Samuel, "that is the best reason I can think of for wanting to come to this place. Tram-bam-bu must be stopped."

"Yes," said Rascal with a smile. "And with your huge size you can easily destroy Tram-bam-bu and all of the other Prehistoric Mice too."

Shaking his head, Samuel said, "No, my friend, there is a better way. You and your friends meet me in my cave tonight and I will tell you."

Rascal was intrigued. His mind was imagining what kind of devilish plot Samuel must have in mind to destroy the Prehistoric Mice. Excited, he made his way back to his friends and soon managed to find them. He told them all about Samuel, and they agreed to go with Rascal to meet him in his cave that night.

It was a dark and rainy night. With wet tails, Rascal and the others went to meet Samuel. In the cave they soon discovered they were in the company of about one hundred other unknown to them cats, and also a few familiar ones that they had met before: Mau, What-What, and Marmalade. To the surprise of Samuel and all other cats they danced together the dance of old friends meeting again, the dance of happiness, and the dance of friendship. It was so spontaneous they did not even realize when they started to dance.

"This results from great happiness," said Rascal.

"And for the threads that pull us together," said Mau, with sincerity.

"For a chat about politics," said Marmalade and smiled. What-What just nodded his head.

"I am so glad to have invited positive cats," said Samuel, happily.

Samuel, the Prehistoric Cat, sat in the middle of his cave and said, "This is the first lesson: Joy and Good Humor! It is most important for a cat to always be smiling, content and cheerful. Be always happy because happiness attracts more happiness. Smiling and good humor are healing – not only for you, but for everyone who stands in your field of purring. Humor is very contagious and soon there will be more happy and healthy cats in this world."

When the Prehistoric Cat finished his speech, a

small sad-faced cat came to Rascal and joyfully said, "If you'd like to go fishing one day, I can take you with me. I'm Fishing Cat, I came from Nepal. I'm a very good diver." He told Rascal how he loves to dive into the water and swim underwater to grab fish with his mouth. Rascal was amazed at how wonderful it must be to have such ability.

A second cat came to Rascal and said, "I like to eat frogs, but only tree frogs. I'm Margay, a spotted cat from Mexico." This spotted cat had a long tail and was an accomplished climber. He and his kind could run up and down the trees like a squirrel, almost never falling. Rascal was intrigued but he wasn't so impressed by Margay's diet: insects, fruits and tree frogs. None of that even comes close to tuna, Rascal thought.

Meanwhile Samuel, the Prehistoric Cat, was explaining to the group gathered before him why he did not want to harm Tram-bam-bu, the Prehistoric Mouse. He had another idea. He told them that if he used force to kill her it would attract the Prehistoric Dogs, who would kill the Prehistoric Cats, and then the Prehistoric Bears would hunt the Prehistoric Dogs, and on it would go... Samuel's idea was to use power, instead of force. Force is limited and is always opposing another force, he taught them. Power is unlimited. It comes from within, and does not create enemies or anything negative. It is only here to stay and to attract. So, Samuel advised that all cats all over the world should simply purr, and by the "magic of purring", bad mice would be changed to good, or at the very least, they would be disarmed. This power of purring would not cause any anger or bad feelings. According to Samuel, it was the purr-fect solution to their problem.

\*\*\*

The very next day, Rascal and his friends stealthily made their way into the camp of the Prehistoric Mice. From behind a huge banana tree, they watched as the gigantic mice, twice the size of ordinary cats, went about their business. "This is not good," Bunny said. "Let us flee before we are all killed!"

But Lumby, never having seen such gigantic mice, thought they must be some kind of toys. He dashed out from behind their hiding place and waltzed right up to the leader of the Prehistoric Mice, Tram-bam-bu. The kitten smiled as he looked up at the enormous mouse. "Gee," he said, "you look just like the big mouse that the Prehistoric Cat told us about."

Laughing hard, Tram-bam-bu said, "Yeah, right! Ha. Ha ha ha ha. Prehistoric Cats do not exist!"

Philosopher urged, "Are we all cowards? We must go and save our little friend before he is devoured."

Rascal lowered his eyes and began to purr. He was purring, and purring, and purring. Remembering Samuel's lecture about purring power the other cats soon joined Rascal in a uniform purring concert.

After a short time Tram-bam-bu, who was ready

to pounce on Lumby, suddenly stopped and said, "Go to your cats, they must be concerned for you. And the next time you come to the Enchanted Forest, don't look for Prehistoric Birds! Ha ha ha ha. Leave now, before I change my mind!" And she let him go.

She also freed the tiny white mouse's mother, Bala; her two sisters, Cala, and Dala; and all the other ordinary-sized mice she had enslaved. They were so overjoyed at being freed that – with no fear at all – they ran right up to the cats, and thanked them over and over again. Bala promised them gifts of cheese every year for life. "For all nine of your lives," Cala and Dala said at the same time. Now, the cats didn't love cheese as much as the mice... but it was a nice gesture anyway.

*** 

As Lumby scampered back to rejoin the group, the tails of the rest of the cats formed question marks. They were very confused and they had lots of questions.

"That huge mouse could have swallowed the poor little kitten," said Bunny in amazement. "Instead, she indeed let him go! And the servant mice too!" The other cats remained likewise perplexed.

Then Rascal reminded them about Samuel's idea. His brother's eyes lit up. "It is so simple!" shouted Philosopher "Nobody will forbid purring. We must do this more! This is just the beginning, don't you see? They are just beginning to trust us!"

The two brothers insisted to stay and purr all night, hoping to make a lasting peace with the Prehistoric Mice. But the others were too afraid to do that.

"We must leave this place while we still can," Sofia cried.

"I have to agree," said Bunny. "I don't know why those gigantic mice let us go, but I am not going to be the cat that got killed by curiosity!"

The others were ready to flee in a panic, and Rascal knew that he and his brother could not stop them.

"Listen to me!" Rascal shouted over all of their bickering. "Wise old Samuel has shown us the way. Running away is for cowards. Fighting is for warmongers. We are not either of those things. We are cats, and we know a better way. The way of peace. You just have to give it a chance."

"Very wise, my brother," Philosopher said smiling.

But the others still let the fear in their hearts rule over their minds. They refused to follow. Some wanted to go back to the safety of Samuel's cave. Others wanted to leave the Enchanted Forest altogether and return to the delightful valley from where they came. The only thing they could agree on... was to disagree.

As they argued amongst themselves, Bala, the mother mouse, climbed up on Rascal's back so that all of the cats could see her. Rascal didn't seem to mind it at all. In fact, he was curious to hear what she had to say. "Please, my new friends, please listen to me," she shouted. "I know that you are cats and we are mice, but you saved me and my daughters and for that I am in your debt."

With her words, the noisy cats quieted down.

"I know you can't decide what to do next, and where you should go," Bala said. "However, when we return to our village there will be a great celebration for our safe return. We would like for all of you to come with us as our honored guests."

There was loud meowing as the cats agreed to go with her.

\*\*\*

As the group followed the mice back to their home village of Cheddarville, Rascal and his brother were in a deep discussion over the events they had just seen. "Philosopher, there's something I don't understand," said Rascal.

"And what would that be?" curiously asked Philosopher.

They passed several gigantic trees as they walked along and talked. Some of them looked like palm trees, others like pines and still others like overgrown bushes. It was amazing to see so many different kinds of plants all so close together. The trail they were on was narrow and winding, but the agile mice were scurrying along quite quickly for such tiny creatures. The cats followed closely behind, many of them engaged in friendly conversations with the little rodents.

Rascal continued, "Why is it that our fellow cats are so willing to make friends with these ordinary mice, yet not with the Prehistoric Mice?"

Philosopher scratched a flea from behind his ear before answering. "I will tell you why. It is because of fear."

Rascal leaped over a big rut in the road, then looked at his brother with a question in his eyes. "I don't know what you mean by that," he said. "What about fear? We have nothing to fear from these ordinary mice."

"Ahh," said Philosopher, "that is true. "But what about the Prehistoric Mice?"

"Yes," said Rascal, "now I know what you mean. The others have no problems making friends with those that are smaller then them. Since they know the ordinary mice cannot hurt them, they have nothing to fear from them and therefore they can be their friends."

"That's right," said Philosopher. "What else?"

Without missing a beat, Rascal picked up right where he left off. "But the Prehistoric Mice are bigger than us, so we are afraid of them and don't want to be their friends."

"Exactly," said Philosopher. "Yet, these ordinary mice should be afraid of us, but they are not. Why do you think that is?"

Rascal did not know the answer to his brother's riddle. But before he got a chance to ponder it, his nose began to quiver in the air. The other cats were sensing something different too.

"What is that smell?" asked Sofia, her nose twitching in the air.

"Cheese!" shouted Lumby, and dashed ahead of the others to catch up with the lead mice, Bala, Cala, and Dala.

\*\*\*

They had arrived in Cheddarville, the home village of the mice. It was hidden amongst the dense trees of the Enchanted Forest. The village had a central square where the mice did most of their business and shopping. The streets were incredibly clean, with no litter at all. This was very different from what the cats had expected. All of their lives they had heard of the ways that mice lived, and all that they had heard had always been negative. Mice were said to be dumb, dirty and lazy. But nothing could be further from the truth. Their little village was immaculate. Beyond the central business district there was a school, hospital and beautiful tree-lined streets with tiny houses that the mice lived in.

The one characteristic they had always heard about mice that did turn out to be true, however, was their incredible appetite for cheese. And this aptly named town confirmed what they already knew. There was cheese everywhere. You could smell it even as you approached the gates of the town. Once inside, a visitor would immediately notice all of the beautiful little wine and cheese shops, not to mention the gigantic cheese factory, and even little cars made out of Swiss cheese, with holes for windows.

"Welcome to our town," Bala proclaimed as she led them through the main gates. "We have never had cats here before, I must confess, but somebody had to be first, and I am glad that it is all of you."

That night the mice put on a huge feast in honor of the heroic cats who had rescued their leader and her children. The cats ate more cheese in that one night than they had in their entire lives (maybe even in all nine lives, Rascal joked). There were cheese sandwiches, grilled cheese, ham and cheese, cheese omelets, crackers and cheese, cheese dip, cheese popcorn, even cheese flavored soda.

Everybody had a great time. There was singing and dancing, jokes were told, and friendships were made. It was as if they had all known each other forever. It was a night none of them would ever forget. After so many years of fighting, the cats and mice had finally come to realize that it was more fun to party together.

\*\*\*

Meanwhile, back in the pleasant valley where Rascal

and his friends came from, there was great concern for the small group of cats that were missing. Especially worried was Dandy, a fashionable black cat with a smattering of white under his jaw, and his wife Snow, known for her beautiful snow white fur.

"It has been days since anyone has seen them," Snow said anxiously.

"Yes," agreed Dandy, "I am getting worried too. We need to put together a search party to find them."

A cat named Nasty, who had never been friendly to anybody, especially not to Rascal, laughed his high pitch laugh. "Why should we be worried about that bunch of fools? I'm sure they have wandered off again and gotten themselves into more trouble. Let them pay for their own foolishness."

"Well," said Dandy, "I don't know how you can be so cruel to a fellow cat."

"Yes," agreed his wife Snow. "And you know the rumors, Nasty. They say that Rascal and the others were last seen near the border with the Enchanted Forest."

"Which means they might be in great danger," added Dandy. "Let's go, my wife, we will search on our own if these cowards are too afraid to go with us."

Now this got the attention of Nasty's two companions – Clumsy, who was practically his shadow, and Black Claw, a big cat that most of the others were afraid of. "We are not afraid of anything," insulted Black Claw said.

"That's right," chimed in Clumsy. "I mean, that IS right, isn't it, Nasty?"

The truth was, Nasty was very afraid, in fact terrified, to even go near the Enchanted Forest. But he couldn't let his friends see that. He always thought of himself as their leader, and he wanted them to believe that he was tough and not afraid of anything. He leaped up onto a rock and said, "Me, afraid? Ha! Come, I will lead all of you into the Enchanted Forest!"

As the group set off for the mysterious woods they all had heard about, but none of them had ever entered, they cautiously made their way to the edge of the valley. Snow and Dandy went first, then Black Claw and Clumsy. Their "leader," Nasty, took up the rear. "Just to make sure none of you decide to chicken out and go home," he explained.

\*\*\*

Back in Cheddarville, as everyone was relaxing after the huge feast, Bala sat down in her favorite chair and all of the cats gathered around her. She began to tell them the story of what life was like when she and her daughters were the servants of the Prehistoric Mice.

"For those of us who were forced to serve the Prehistoric Mice, we had to live by their rules. And their rules all revolved around their calendar."

"What's a calendar?" asked Lumby.

"It is a way of keeping track of time," said Bunny.

"Why would anyone want to do that?" Lumby said, dumfounded. "Time doesn't run on a track. Only trains do."

They all laughed at the youngster's naivety, and then Bala continued with her story.

"You see, for the Prehistoric Mice, Monday was the Day of Apathy. On this day they would always feel nothing but despair and hopelessness. The world and the future always looked bleak. I remember how they would stare blankly into the corners of their caves, not saying a word. They had lost the will to live."

"That is terrible," said Philosopher sadly. "I cannot imagine living such a way."

"Yet that is the way it is with them," said Bala. "They do everything with such apathy that in the end they can do nothing. It is why they kidnapped ordinary mice like me and my children to do all their chores for them. Their apathy made them too lazy to do anything for themselves. They couldn't even get up in the morning without three of us servant mice making a big loud racket, banging pots and pans, blowing whistles, doing anything just to wake them up."

"It's hard to imagine that anyone could be that lazy," remarked Rascal.

"That's what I thought too, at first," Bala explained. "But then I realized that these Prehistoric Mice had learned these bad, lazy habits from their parents, the Pre-Prehistoric Mice. And once they had servants to do all of their work, it almost seemed useless for them to even wake up in the morning. The apathy got so bad that they even needed their servants to help them get dressed, cook their meals, even to lift the spoons to their mouths! Yes, they were a lazy bunch indeed. At least on Mondays."

Next, Bala told them about Tuesdays...

"Tuesday was the Day of Guilt. The Prehistoric Mice felt guilty because of yesterday's apathy and they stayed inside their caves all morning. So once again it was the servant mice that had to do all of the work.

"I remember one Tuesday when Tram-bam-bu broke a mirror and she cried all day with guilt and shame. Then she said she felt guilty for being too fat. Her daughter was ashamed because of having too many blond hairs, and her son was ashamed because of having too many black hairs on his neck. They were also ashamed of their nationality – Prehistoric.

The one thing they did not seem to feel guilty about was enslaving their fellow mice, just because we were not as big and strong as them. Somehow they seemed to overlook that one.

At night they went to bed, still carrying the shame.

At least on Tuesdays."

Next, Bala told them about Wednesdays...

"I remember how sad I always was on Wednesdays," said Bala, a tear forming in her eye.

"Why was that day so sad?" asked Bunny with

genuine concern in his voice.

"It's Because Wednesday was the Day of Grief," Bala explained. "All of the Prehistoric Mice would grieve because of yesterday's guilt and shame. They would even skip breakfast. At dinner they were in still deeper grief because they had not eaten breakfast. I remember that Tram-bam-bu was in grief about her husband being in the Arctic. Then she was in grief because of the extinction of the dinosaurs, cave bears, dire wolves, and the woolly mammoths. After supper the grief grew even more because she was not as famous as she wanted to be. And because the whole world did not look and think just like mice, which was what she wanted above all.

At night, the Prehistoric Mice went to bed grieving. Even their dreams, sad to say, were filled with nothing but grief and sadness.

At least on Wednesdays."

Next, Bala told them about Thursdays…

"One of the worst days of the week," she explained, "was Thursday. For Thursday was the Day of Fear. From the time they woke up, Tram-bam-bu and her children were afraid that they would die someday, which of course they knew would come at some point. But rather than looking forward to a blessed reward when they die, as we ordinary mice do, they just sat around and worried in fear."

"Given their awful behavior, perhaps they were afraid they would receive punishment rather than a reward," Philosopher opined.

"Perhaps," said Bala. "But whatever their reason, it made life quite difficult for all of us servant mice. Every Thursday we would do all that we could trying to comfort them. The house mice that lived in the attic of the library read lots of books. They tried to reason with the Prehistoric Mice about their fear of death. They said, 'Just as we are born, so shall we also die. Your future has already been decided in that respect. So instead of living with fear, isn't it better to spend your life doing what you like? Besides, when a mouse dies, her invisible body (spirit) goes into another small mouse and so on.'

For a few minutes that would make the Prehistoric Mice feel better, but then they would think up of something else to be afraid of. For example, they would worry about floods, fires, earthquakes... All sorts of natural disasters. We would explain to them that these things were just part of nature, and worrying about a tornado, for instance, does not make one less likely to happen. But they did not want to listen to reason. No, not at all. They only wanted to listen to their fears...

At least on Thursdays."

Next, Bala told them about Fridays...

"This was the worst day for us poor small mice," she said. "Friday was the Day of Anger. Pamparamba wanted to have a swing, but the small mice couldn't make it, so he was very angry. Tumbaramba wanted to have a dress made from the morning fog interlaced with spring wildflowers. She was angry at spring and at flowers because it was summer. Tram-bam-bu was angry because she saw three gray hairs on her tail and two wrinkles on her face. She was angry with her husband because he was away, and also because he did nothing but teach Arctic mice. Then all of them were angry because trees are green, the sky is blue and the sun is bright."

"Didn't they realize that anger never solves anything," said Philosopher, wondering how such powerful creatures could be so ignorant.

"No," replied Bala, "they never realized that. Because they were too busy being angry.

At least on Fridays."

Finally, Bala told them about Saturdays...

"Saturday was the Day of Pride," Bala told the cats assembled around her. "Tram-bam-bu wanted to have her bedroom decorated with the petals of wild roses, so she would send her servants off into the forest to look for them. When they came back with the petals, and beautifully decorated her bedroom, Tram-bam-bu felt so proud that she made our finest sculptors build a huge bronze statue of her and place it in the center of their village."

Rascal said, "But how could she take pride in anything when all of her accomplishments came at the expense of ordinary mice?"

"That's an excellent question," Bala said. "And one that I must have asked myself hundred of times.

At least on Saturdays."

\*\*\*

The next morning, they all decided that the best plan was to go back to Samuel and ask for more advice. On the now familiar trail to Samuel's cave, Rascal stopped suddenly in his tracks and Lumby sniffed the wind. They heard a suppressed cry for help.

"Somebody is in trouble!" shouted Rascal, running in the direction of the cry. All the others followed in his claw tracks. They came to a beautiful apple orchard where they saw an old water well, unused for many years. Rascal spotted two cats looking down into the well. He immediately recognized them as Snow and Dandy. Rascal said, "Snow. Dandy. What are you doing here?"

"We came to find you," Dandy explained.

"We were worried sick about you," his wife Snow added.

Dandy told Rascal and the others the rest of the story. "When we did not find you the first night, Nasty said that you were not worth wasting any more time on, and he decided to turn back. Of course, his two stooges – Clumsy and Black Claw – followed him. But apparently they got separated in the darkness. My cat intuition told me that the other two made it home, but I knew Nasty was in trouble. So Snow and I went looking for him, and that is when we discovered that Nasty fell down into this well."

"We have to help him," Rascal said.

"After all he has done to you?" said Dandy. "I

would think you would just want to let him die."

"Yes, let him stay there forever," added Sofia.

"Help. Please," pleaded Nasty. "Please help me get out of this well."

Lumby was dancing around the well, a joyful dance of new play. He thought that Nasty was having lots of fun sitting down there.

Bunny looked around at all the cats and said, "We should not be revengeful. It is better to forgive."

"He is right," said Rascal. "If I hold a grudge, then I would be the one who is truly nasty. Then he shouted down into the well, "We're going to help you, Nasty, but first we have to figure out how."

He scanned the area, and then he spotted a long branch.

"Aha!" Rascal exclaimed. "That's it. We can use this long branch to get him out. Come and help me, all of you."

The other cats dragged the heavy branch over to the well and then, using all of their combined strength, they pushed it over the side of the well and held it as it dangled down from the top. Then they began slowly lowering it down.

"Nasty!" Rascal shouted down into the well. "We are lowering a branch for you to climb up and out of there. Grab hold of it."

"It's… it's too dark in here!" came Nasty's frightened voice. "I can't see anything! Where is this branch? I cannot see it."

"You'll have to move around and feel for it in the

darkness," Rascal shouted down into the well.

"I... I am too... too...," they all heard Nasty say.

"'Too' what? Tell us!" Dandy demanded.

"I am too afraid," Nasty finally admitted. "I am perched on a ledge about halfway down the well. If I try to reach for the branch and I fall, I will plunge into even more darkness and you will never be able to reach me. Oh, this is all my fault! I have been so cruel my whole life, and now I am going to be left abandoned in this awful well forever!" he wailed.

Rascal felt pity for Nasty, despite all the mean things Nasty had done to him in the past. Now all he wanted to do was to help the desperate cat. But he didn't know how.

Philosopher moved his right ear to the front, his left ear to the back and closed his eyes. Rascal knew his brother was thinking, and so did the others. They all remained silent.

After a while, they heard Nasty's voice rise up from the well again. "What are you doing up there? " he asked. "Please don't leave!"

Philosopher did not respond, but only moved his left ear to the front and his right ear to the back, then said, "Please do not bother me now."

"What are you doing?" demanded Nasty.

"I'm thinking."

"How long will you think?"

"It depends on my thoughts," said Philosopher seriously. "From time to time I have very deep thoughts, deep like the bottom of the ocean. Those thoughts I have to consider carefully. At that time I sit without movement and meditate."

"How long will it be?" groaned the voice from the well.

"Once I did disentangle some very difficult problem within six months."

"Think faster! I command you! It mean... Please...," said Nasty.

"Do not hustle me. The free spirit of a philosopher like me does not like to be rushed."

Rascal looked into the well and said to Nasty, "Do not worry. We will be back tomorrow and will try to help you somehow."

"Mercy!"

"If it is very important to you to get out of this well, I will try to find some idea," said Philosopher.

"How long it will be?"

"I don't know yet because it is a very difficult task, but I think... three weeks, maybe four..."

"Please, do not joke, the storm is coming and I'm afraid of rain... and there is no place to hide."

Rascal looked up into sky. Bunny looked to the forest and Lumby smelled the air.

"That's right!" shouted the cats and Sofia pointed to the black cloud that was quickly covering the blue sky.

"Let's go find the owner of this well and bring him here," said Rascal looking for a house. In the distance he saw a wooden fence slanted with age and an old wooden house half-hidden among the trees.

Philosopher looked behind him and said with melancholy, "I wish I were in my home now. I would be reclined in my wicker basket with my stomach up. I would sleep, and when not sleeping I would eat, then sleep again and eat, and so on for a hundred years."

Rascal sighed as loud as the blowing wind.

The cats quickly ran to the wooden shed and arrived just as the first big drops of rain hit the ground, followed by lightning.

\*\*\*

"We are lucky," meowed Rascal.

"It's a pity that Nasty..." started Bunny.

"Don't pity him, this rain is good for him," said Sofia, jokingly.

"Revenge is not good," said Bunny.

"It is not our revenge. It is nature's revenge," said Philosopher with a grin, and added, "I did not push him to this well and I did not send the rain. Still, he knows now what it means for a cat to be wet."

"We are not guilty for what's happened to Nasty," said Rascal. "Nature has certain laws. If somebody does something bad to somebody else, it will surely come back to him, even if he does not believe in that or does not realize that. Take for example the law of gravity! It exists and it works even if somebody does not believe in it." Rascal jumped high, then landed on the ground to show how the law of gravity works.

"What is it?" asked Lumby.

Bunny patiently explained that it is an invisible force that keeps all cats from flying off into space.

"When the branch that you're sitting on breaks, you will land down, not up," added Philosopher.

\*\*\*

After the storm subsided and the sky became blue again, the cats went to the old wooden house. It looked uninhabited. The roof was in bad condition and the paint on the wooden stairs was peeling off. There were cracks in the walls and the Morning Glory was trying to take over the house, reaching up to the chimney. The rain pipes were not working. The door was ajar.

"Which one of us will go and ask for help?" asked Rascal.

"I will go," answered Lumby quickly.

"Okay, you go and we will secure you from behind in case of an emergency," said Rascal.

"This house is very sorrowful," said Snow with a sigh.

"We should not go there," added Sofia.

"Come in," said a voice.

"Run!" shouted Dandy.

"Wait! Nobody will harm you," continued the voice.

"We do not trust you," said Rascal protecting Lumby with his body.

"Do not be afraid! I swear on all cats. Why do

you not believe me?"

In the threshold appeared a blind yellow cat named Oscar.

Rascal said sadly, "It is a very sorrowful house that nobody lives in."

"How can you say nobody lives here? Grandma lives here with me. And flies are habitual guests; rheumatism and sometimes the flu visits us," said Oscar, the blind cat with a smile. "I'm very happy for your visit because for a long time I have not spoken with any cats. Nobody comes here. Only Grandma lives here on her very poor pension. Come in and eat, then go about your business."

"We need help to get Nasty out of the well," said Rascal.

"Grandma is too old and frail to help you," said the blind yellow cat, "and as I cannot see, I doubt I could help you much either."

Rascal thought for a moment. Then, as if a light bulb went off in his head, he said, "That's it! I have an idea. Oscar, you cannot see, is that not correct?"

"Yes, I have been a blind cat all my life," he answered. "Why are you asking that? Are you making fun of me?"

Rascal noticed that old Oscar was arching his back in anger. He did not mean to insult the old cat, but now was not the time to worry over hurt feelings.

"Believe me, Oscar," Rascal said, "I mean no insult. In fact, it is because you cannot see that you are precisely the one that we need to help us."

The blind cat seemed astonished. "Me?" he said. "What can I do? How can I help when all you strong cats with perfect vision can't do anything?"

"Come to the well with us," replied Rascal, "and I will explain everything"

\*\*\*

Together, Philosopher and Rascal guided Oscar over to the long tree branch that the other cats were once again holding down into the well. Rascal said, "Now here is what I want you to do, Oscar. Since you have spent a lifetime of learning to live in the darkness, you, better than any of us, should be able to shimmy down this branch into the well to help get Nasty out."

"Oh, I am not sure…" Oscar was stammering. "I have never done anything like this before. It is such a great responsibility. Nobody has ever trusted me to do an important job before."

"My good cat," Philosopher said, "there is a first time for everything."

And with that encouragement, Oscar bravely leapt onto the side of the well. The others were amazed at his agility.

"How could you know where you are jumping if you are blind," Bunny asked.

"Years of practice," Oscar explained. "I used to play on this well when I was a kitten. I came to know its every nook and cranny, and I guess there are some things you just never forget."

As he spoke he was nimbly descending into the dark well. Except, of course, to him it wasn't any darker than it had always been, anyway. When he was about 40 feet down he reached out his paw and grabbed hold of Nasty. "Gotcha!" triumphed Oscar.

They all cheered as they pulled Oscar back up with a very relieved-looking Nasty clinging to him for dear life.

After the two clambered over the side of the well, Rascal was shocked when Nasty ran up to him and gave him a tight embrace (the cat equivalent of a bear hug).

"I owe you my life Rascal," murmured Nasty.

Rascal felt embarrassed by all of the praise that his old nemesis was heaping on him. "Oh, it was nothing," he said. "I'm sure you would have done the same thing for me." Actually, he wasn't so sure, but it seemed like the right thing to say.

They all thanked Oscar, too, for without his assistance and his bravery they would have never been able to rescue Nasty. The blind old cat said, "I must go tell Grandma of this great adventure. She will be so excited!" And with those words he dashed back home.

\*\*\*

The happy group was standing around the well talking when all of a sudden they heard a strange voice calling from the edge of a nearby field. "Over here! Over here!" the voice was yelling.

They looked all around and didn't see a thing, until finally Sofia exclaimed, "Look, it's our little mouse friend, Bala!"

But Bala was not there on a social call. Her voice sounded alarmed. "You are in great danger. Run over here! Quickly!"

None of the cats sensed any danger as they looked all about them. "This is silly," said Bunny, "I don't see... say, Lumby, why are you looking up in the sky?"

They all craned their necks backwards to see what the kitten was looking at up in the blue, cloudless sky. And that is when they saw it.

"I... I... I don't believe my eyes," Sofia stuttered.

"You better believe them," said startled Philosopher, "for no two cats see the same delusion... and I am seeing what you see!"

Indeed, all of them saw it, soaring high above them. It was a gargantuan sized bird, with a wingspan so huge it blotted out the sunlight. As the darkness swept over them, Bala's voice, soft yet firm, urged them on. "He has spotted you! Run to me, over here! I will hide you!"

The cats did not need any more convincing. All of them ran as fast as their four paws would take them in Bala's direction.

Overhead, the massive bird had indeed spotted

them. It flapped its mighty wings faster, pointed its enormous head downward and swooped into a blazingly fast dive, screeching loudly as it closed in on them.

As the cats, using every ounce of their strength, reached the edge of the field, Bala pointed to a hole in the ground. "Hurry, get in! You will be safe in here."

It was a mouse hole, the kind that the mice used for protection from all kinds of hunters, especially cats. It was very small, but the nimble cats all managed to get inside. All of them, that is, except for Philosopher. He was a little bit heavier than the others, and as he tried to squeeze himself into the hole he got stuck.

Beneath him, all the others were safely inside the elaborate tunnel complex the mice had built. They could see Philosopher's feet dangling above them, but his mid section was tightly lodged in the hole's entrance.

Philosopher could see the giant bird closing in on him, the distance shortening with each flap of its powerful wings. He tried to keep his voice calm, but it wasn't easy. "I could use some help, my friends," he called. "Pull on me with all your might. I only have a few seconds!"

"I have an idea," Rascal suddenly said. "Lumby, please give me that bucket of cheese popcorn you've been dragging along."

"But it's empty," the kitten said. "I only kept it as

a Cheddarville souvenir. All that's left is a bunch of grease on the bottom."

"Exactly!" replied Rascal, grabbing the bucket.

Confused Lumby released the bucket and Rascal quickly dipped his paw into the grease, then reached up and smeared it around his brother's stuck midsection. The slippery liquid did its job immediately and Philosopher, with one last great push, was able to force himself through the hole and down into the tunnel.

It was just in the nick of time, too, for no sooner was Philosopher safely inside the tunnel did the mammoth bird reach the top of the hole. He landed on top of the entrance and, from underneath, the cats – and Bala, the mouse who saved them – could see the bottoms of his huge talons.

"We are all indebted to you forever, Bala," said Rascal. "You saved all of our lives with your bravery."

"You owe me nothing," said Bala. "Doing nice things to each other – even when it's risky – is what being friends is all about."

They all waited for an hour until the frustrated bird finally moved off the hole. He walked around the field searching for prey, but was unable to find any. Tired, the king-sized bird sat down on the ground and fell fast asleep.

***

Down inside the tunnel, Lumby was getting bored. When the others weren't watching, he climbed up out of the hole and observed, in awe, the giant bird sleeping about ten yards away. His kitten curiosity got the best of him and he slowly approached the strange creature. Gently he climbed up onto one of his wings, then, tiptoeing lightly, made his way to the top of the bird's head. "Wow," he whispered to himself. "I wish my friends could see me now. What great fun this is."

Back inside the tunnel, Bala was explaining to the cats that the Prehistoric Birds were very rare. "We only see them once a year. We think it is the season when they migrate to the other side of the world."

They all listened fascinated as she continued her speech, when suddenly Snow said, "Hey, where is Lumby?"

They all looked around but nobody could see him. Then, from the hole's entrance, Bunny shouted, "Holy cats! You won't believe where I found him! He's perched on top of that monster's head!"

They all rushed to the hole's entrance and scrambled up and out onto the surface. "Oh my! What are we going to do?" Sofia wailed.

"We have to go get him," said Rascal. "I will go."

"No, I will do it," opposed Philosopher.

Then Bunny volunteered. And Snow and Dandy.

And Sofia. All of them said they would go to rescue the helpless little kitten. Even Nasty!

"While we stay here and argue, that bird is going to wake up," said Philosopher in exasperation.

"Then let's all go," decided Rascal.

\*\*\*

And that's exactly what they did. Quietly, with the sure-footed agility cats are so well known for, the group made its way up onto the wings and body of the huge, sleeping Prehistoric Bird. However, they didn't want to walk onto his head where Lumby was playfully dancing around. They were afraid that with their extra weight they would wake the bird up.

They all tried to get Lumby's attention by whispering to him. "Lumby, come down quickly, it is very dangerous up there," said Philosopher, who was standing the closest to the kitten, just a few feet away.

But Lumby was too busy dancing and having fun to hear him. He liked closing his eyes as he danced, losing himself in his mirth, so he didn't even notice that all of his friends were now on top of the bird too, trying to coax him down.

Suddenly, Bunny said, "Wh... What's that? It feels like the earth is moving!"

And indeed it was. They were all knocked down as the massive bird stood up, awoken from his slumber. Lumby slid down the bird's ten-foot neck and landed at Philosopher's feet. "What are you doing here, Philosopher?" the kitten asked innocently. "Did you come to play with me?"

Before the wise cat could reply, all of them felt themselves being lifted off the ground. Unaware of his uninvited guests, the Prehistoric Bird had begun flapping his wings and immediately took off into the air. The terrified cats huddled together on the giant bird's back.

* * *

Soon they were thousands of feet above the ground. The wind rushed past them as the bird picked up the speed. Once they realized that they were not going to fall off, they stopped worrying and just enjoyed the ride.

"This is most amazing food for thought," remarked a wide-eyed Philosopher. "We are seeing things that I'm sure no other cat has ever seen before."

"That's true," replied his brother. "The highest any cat has ever been is the top of tallest tree. Now we can see the tops of the trees far beneath us."

As the bird surged forward, the view was indeed breathtaking. Beneath them they could see for miles and miles. At first it was mostly forest, with some scattered villages here and there. They could see the thatched rooftops of primitive huts and also the towers of great castles and fortresses. They huddled together as they sailed through the sky at tremendous speed.

"Look at that!" shouted Lumby.

The group turned its attention to where the kitten was pointing. They now witnessed an awesome sight looming in front of them. Water. Miles and miles of water. And then more water. The startled cats had never seen anything like that.

"What is it?" asked Snow and Dandy in unison.

"I have read about this in my books," replied Philosopher. "I believe it is what they call an ocean. There are four of them, and they connect all of the far-flung lands of the Earth. With their vast expanses of empty open water they can be used to separate people. Or, on the other hand, by peaceful exploration with sailing ships, the oceans can be a wonderful way to bring people together."

The others didn't fully understand what Philosopher was trying to tell them. None of them had ever seen an ocean before, not to mention a ship. Still, they found the shimmering water, and the whitecaps on the waves, mesmerizing. They stared in wonderment as they flew above the ocean depths for hours. In fact, none of them were even sure how much time had passed.

"It is indeed beautiful down there, but it seems a shame to me to have such a large place where no living thing can find a home," Rascal said.

Laughing, Philosopher answered, "Oh, you have so much to learn, my brother. There are many creatures that live in the ocean."

Confused, Rascal asked, "There are? Like what?"

Remembering what he had read in his books, Philosopher said, "Giant creatures known as whales, for example. They live in the ocean, but they breathe air just like you and me."

"Ha!" said Sofia. "Now I know you are telling a tall tale, Philosopher. How could such a creature live in the ocean and yet breathe air like you and me? It is not possible. It would drown."

"Ah," replied Philosopher, "there are answers that nature has that neither you nor I would come up with, my good Sofia. You see, whales have something called a blowhole on the top of their heads. They rise up out of the ocean and spray water high into the air. Then they fill their enormous lungs with air. It is a process called…"

Before he could finish his detailed lesson on the physiology of whales, Rascal asked, "OK, so what other kinds of creatures live in the oceans?"

Philosopher thought for a moment. "Well," he said, "there is a strange beast with eight arms known as an octopus. And there are creatures that carry an electric charge like lightning. They are called eels. There are also seals, dolphins, porpoises, and of course, all kinds of fish."

"Fish!" chimed in Lumby. "I'm starving, let's dive into that ocean down there and get some fish!"

The kitten moved to the edge of the great bird and prepared to leap over its side. Rascal grabbed him at the last possible moment. "My little friend, it is thousands of feet down to the ocean. You cannot jump. You would be killed."

Lumby looked confused. He cocked his head to one side. "What does 'killed' mean?" he asked.

Before Rascal could answer him, Nasty shouted, "Look down there! I can't believe what I'm seeing!"

Then they all saw what Nasty saw. They were now past the ocean and over land again. There were gigantic creatures – even bigger than the Prehistoric Bird they were riding on – tromping on the face of the earth. The fearsome looking animals were covered with scales that looked like armor plating. Some of them were green, others were brown. All of them had eyes that seemed too tiny for their massive heads.

"What the heck are those things," inquired Rascal, turning to his brother.

"They are dinosaurs," replied Philosopher. "The word means 'terrible lizard.' But I thought Tram-bam-bu said they were extinct." The wise cat seemed disturbed that he was looking at something that he could not understand or explain.

The Prehistoric Bird obviously spotted the dinosaurs too, and they apparently made him nervous. He flapped his powerful wings even more strongly and lifted up even higher into the sky.

"I think he's trying to get away from them by flying into that big cloud up ahead," said Dandy.

He was right. That was exactly what the frightened bird was trying to do. But before he could reach the safety of the cloud, one of the dinosaurs, a particularly ferocious looking creature with a long green neck, spotted him. A stream of flame shot out of the dinosaur's nostrils and reached up into the sky, striking the fleeing bird in his tail, which immediately caught fire.

"We're all doomed," Sofia cried. "If this bird crashes, we will crash with him. Even if we survive, those dinosaurs will get us!"

The injured bird was now spinning out of control. Despite his best efforts and furious flapping of the wings, he was going down fast. The fire was spreading, and the huge bird screeched in pain as he continued to burn.

"Listen, all of you!" shouted Rascal. "I have a plan that can save our lives, but we have to act fast. Look at me and do as I do. With all of your strength!"

Rascal ran toward the bird's tail, nimbly holding on to feathers as the bird continued to plummet from the sky. He turned his back toward the bird's tail and started wagging his tail as fast as he could. The others rushed over and they all started wagging too. The great wind that was created, added to the rushing wind from the bird's fall, began to put out the fire.

"Faster!" Rascal cried. "It's almost out!"

They kept wagging. They wagged, then they wagged some more. Faster and faster. The flames were diminishing, but they were not yet completely extinguished. They all started getting tired and their wagging began to slow down.

"Think happy thoughts," Lumby said. "I always

wag my tail faster when I am happy."

He was right. It worked for all of them. The more they focused their minds on happy thoughts, the faster their tails wagged. Some of them thought about food. Others thought about friends. Still others thought about home and family. But all of their thoughts were focused on positive things, whatever it was that made them happy. And before they knew it, their fast wagging tails had put out the fire.

The injured bird regained control of his flight and soon landed in the safety of a nest he had built high up on the side of a lonely cliff, far away from the dinosaurs and from all dangers.

\*\*\*

The cats were startled when they heard the Prehistoric Bird speak for the first time. "My name is Stratosphere," he said. "Do not be frightened. I saw what you did to save me from the dinosaurs. And I will forever be in your debt."

"There is no need to repay us, Mr. Stratosphere," Philosopher said. "A good deed is its own reward. However, you could do me the favor – if you would be so kind – of answering a question that has been vexing me."

"Certainly, my new friend," answered the gigantic bird. "What is it that I can answer for you?"

"I had heard that dinosaurs had become extinct. If that is true, how then did we almost just get turned into roasted cat and bird by one of them?"

Stratosphere's voice was deep and strong, yet surprisingly gentle and soothing. "Well, you are correct in your basic assumption," he said. "At some point in time they did become extinct. But the place we just flew over is called The Land of Time. It is a place where time can be frozen still at any point you wish. We, Prehistoric Birds, fly there once every year, and then we return to the Enchanted Forest. That's way we are rejuvenated every spring. It makes us immortal. Just like the dinosaurs."

What this bird was telling Philosopher was truly amazing. It was hard to believe, yet he was certain it was true. "Can cats travel to The Land of Time too?" Philosopher asked.

The huge bird smiled. "You just did, didn't you?"

Philosopher had to admit that he was right. But the bird's revelation was so stunning that he would have to think about it a little more. No, he would have to think about it a LOT more.

But now it was time for them to return to the Enchanted Forest. They still wanted to meet with Samuel, for they knew there was so much that they could learn from him. Their new friend, Stratosphere, took out some medicine that he had stored in his nest and healed up his tail. Then he was ready to take flight again. The cats gathered together in the middle of his back as he flapped his wings and lifted up over the side of the cliff and into the air again.

A few hours later, Stratosphere landed and they were back in the Enchanted Forest. "This is where I say goodbye to you," the massive bird said.

They had all come to love their new friend, but none of them as much as Philosopher, who admired the great bird for his incredible wisdom. "Will I ever see you again?" the cat asked as he climbed down to the ground.

Stratosphere smiled. "Yes, indeed you will. But whether it will be in this time, or at some time in the past or in the future, well… only time will tell."

With that, he flapped his mighty wings and flew off away from them, out of sight and into the heavens.

*** 

They were back on the trail to Samuel's cave. As they were making their way down the winding trail crossing through some bushes, suddenly Rascal found himself standing – whiskers to whiskers – with a strange cat.

"Who are you? I did not see you yesterday."

"I'm Black Foot Cat," the fierce looking animal said. "I come from the Kalahari Desert in South Africa."

Now, it was well known that these cats were said to be exceptionally fierce. And he looked the part too. The undersides of his feet were black. His coat was yellowish brown but darker on the back, and marked with bold black spots, arranged in rows on the throat, chest and belly. A black line ran across his cheeks from the outer corner of each eye. His ears were reddish brown and slightly rounded.

Rascal was unafraid. He just assumed that he could make friends with everyone. He asked, "What brings you such a long distance, my good fellow, here to this Enchanted Forest?"

Black Foot Cat answered, "I have been invited to Samuel's cave. He is said to be a very wise cat, and we have business to discuss. Very important business."

And so on they went, Black Foot Cat leading the way. Further down the path they met two more cats, Pampas Cat, from the Patagonia desert in Argentina, and Sand Cat, from the Sahara desert in North Africa. These two also traveled halfway around the world for this important meeting with Samuel.

Pampas Cat had big amber eyes. His head was broad with a short muzzle. His ears were pointed, and he was gray black on his back with a silvery white central spot. His legs were short with black bars and spots. His tail was fairly short and bushy, marked with a series of tiny rings.

Sand Cat was one of the smallest of all the wild cats, weighing only a few pounds. His distinctive triangular ears looked too big for the rest of his body. They gave him the ability to hear noises under the sand. As they walked along, Sofia came up beside Sand Cat and said, "So tell me, what does Sand Cat eat?"

In a low sound that almost sounded like barking, Sand Cat answered, "We eat venomous snakes and locusts."

Sofia pointed her nose in the air. "Yum!" she said sarcastically.

\*\*\*

At last they reached Samuel's cave. Samuel and Mau, Marmalade and What-What were already there. Samuel invited the cats for dinner. "Dinner, dinner, cat food cans, cat's cans," shouted Lumby.

Sparks of happiness shone in Samuel's eyes. He said to Lumby, "Welcome, happy small one. You have a big heart. I am glad you feel at home here."

"But not better than in your own home," added Bunny quickly.

Philosopher wanted to know more about purring. He asked whether it is better to purr in the evening or in the morning. The Prehistoric Cat told him it is always the right time to purr. It was an answer that Philosopher liked, because it made him think.

Samuel patiently explained about accepting others as they are. "We have cats, mice, dogs and rabbits. Everyone has to be what they are. That doesn't mean that one is worse or better than another, they are just different. We should accept that mice look like mice, dogs look like dogs, and cats look like cats. Cats eat meat and rabbits eat cabbage. Mice are not better or worse than cats! Each has its own place here in this world, which is like a school for everyone. And everyone has their perfect spot at their class in this school. But Tram-bam-bu does not understand that and she wants to change the world to smell like a mouse, look like a mouse..."

"Let's kill Tram-bam-bu," said Black Foot Cat.

"No!" said Samuel with a voice of authority. "Our task is to purr, and through that purring, make a field of love, acceptance and peace. These cats here are from around the world. They came here to learn how to purr to help themselves and others live happy and peaceful lives."

"Holy Cat!" whispered Rascal.

Some of the other cats did not seem totally convinced. Pampas Cat said, "I did not travel thousands of miles to be told that purring is the way to deal with our enemies! What about the humans? They are quickly taking over the world. How are we supposed to deal with them?"

All the others joined in with their agreement. "Yes, it is the humans who pose the greatest threat," they all told Samuel. "Compared with them, Prehistoric Mouse is just, well, a mouse!"

But the humans, they have tools. And with their big brains they make weapons. Deadly weapons!

Black Foot Cat said, "It is true! I watched in horror once as a group of humans used a new weapon – some sort of stick with a metal tip that flies through the air – to kill one of our cat cousins, the fearsome lion. If they can kill lions, what chance do we have against them?"

As the others clamored and complained, Rascal grew frustrated. He knew that humans were not the enemies of cats. "They are our friends, please believe me," he pleaded with his fellow cats. But they didn't want to hear any of it.

Samuel pulled him aside from the group. "My friend," he whispered, "you are right about humans. There are a few bad ones, but most of them are good. I'm sure they would love cats, maybe even allow us to live with them, if only we would make the first move and show them that we are their friends."

Rascal did not know what to do next. "We passed a camp of humans just a few miles back," he said. "They were all asleep and did not see us. I wanted to stop to say hello, but the other cats were too afraid."

Samuel nodded his wise head and said, "We are all afraid of what we do not know, Rascal. All it takes is one brave cat to lead the way. Now, come, it is time for all of you to rest for the night, for you have all traveled a long way to get here."

*\*\**

That night, as Rascal's companions and all the other cats slept soundly in Samuel's cave Rascal, who only pretended to go to sleep, snuck off on his own. He walked for miles through the dark forest, singing little songs to himself to keep from getting afraid. Cats have excellent night vision and have no problem finding their way in the dark. Shortly after midnight, he reached the camp of humans.

He could see the dwindling remains of a campfire, and several tents. Slowly, he crept toward the entrance of one of the tents, hoping to peer inside. Suddenly, a hand reached out and grabbed him. "Ha! Now I've got you, you little rascal." It was a young girl, she had apparently woken up when she heard Rascal creeping around her tent.

At first Rascal was terrified. Oh no! he thought. Was it true what the others said? Were the humans really cruel monsters? Would they hurt him? Maybe even kill him?

But before he could have another bad thought, the girl began stroking his fur and saying nice words to him. "My brother Hubert will just love you," she whispered.

The cat responded with a gentle purring, which the girl seemed to like very much. She wrapped Rascal up in her arms and brought him with her to her sleeping bag inside the tent, surrounded by her family, most of them snoring. He noticed the name sewn onto the side of her sleeping bag said "Diana." Together, the human and the feline drifted off to sleep.

So Rascal's momentary fears about the humans disappeared. Now he finally had the answer to his brother's riddle that day when they were walking on the trail to Cheddarville. Philosopher had asked then why the small mice were not afraid of the cats, and indeed became their friends. The answer was now as plain to Rascal as the whiskers on his face. The true test of friendship has to do with faith. Faith, that the one who is stronger than you will help you, rather than hurt you. Friends don't become friends because they fear you, but just because they feel love for you. The mice had that kind of faith in the cats, after witnessing their kindness. Now Rascal had that kind of faith in the humans for the very same reason.

He had been right about them all along. Though cats and humans were different, it was just like Samuel had said about the difference between cats and mice, and dogs and cats, and fish and...well, about every living creature. Each one of them had an important place on this beautiful planet called Earth. Each one of them had their own song to sing. And humans did love cats after all. As long as cats gave them the chance...

\*\*\*

Slowly, from somewhere deep inside of himself, Rascal woke up. He was back in the attic, curled up in his favorite cabinet drawer, and it was dark.

He rubbed the sleep off his eyes and looked at the clock at the wall. It was 9:09, cats' favorite time that reminded them – twice a day – of their nine lives.

He looked down at his diary on the floor beneath his cabinet drawer. "Oh no, I must have fallen asleep!"

He was just about to leap down to get his diary when Philosopher galloped up the stairs and seized it. "Ah, so your story is ready?" he asked. "Shall I go get the others?"

Rascal took a deep breath. "Well, Philosopher," he said, "it's time that I tell you the truth. You see, I had been thinking and thinking of a great story to tell, but…"

As Rascal was trying to explain himself, Philosopher had begun reading through the diary. "My brother," he said, "this story, 'The Enchanted Forest,' is better than I could have expected. I apologize for not believing in you."

Rascal shook his head. "It, it… it is?" he stammered.

"Why, yes, you have quite an imagination after all," said Philosopher. "But tell me, did all of this really come to you in a dream?"

Rascal thought about his brother's question. He didn't remember writing a word. But he did remember his dream. It was all coming back to him now. And it all seemed so real. Yet, he knew he never really left the attic. Could imagination really be that powerful? Could it really take him away to far off lands, just like the power of a good book?

"Well, Philosopher," he said, "you like to think all the time and I like to just do stuff. To answer your question, yes, this story did come to me in a dream. Maybe dreams are where we just do the stuff that we think about all the time."

Philosopher scratched his chin with his paw. "You may be right, Rascal," he said. "But I will have to think about it for a while."

Rascal gently took back his diary and happily curled up in his cabinet drawer once again. "That's a great idea, my brother," he said as he closed his eyes for another cat nap. "And while you do that, I will dream another dream...."

THE END

# Answers to Cat Trivia

1. Unfortunately nobody knows how many cats there are in the world but it is known that there are more then 70 million pet cats in America.
2. On average cats sleep 16 hour a day.
3. According to The American Veterinary Medical Association there are about 10 million more cats then dogs in America.

# Why Some Cats are Rascals

## Book 2

## From Cat's Heaven to Cat's Hell

The next story by
### Boszenna Nowiki

*(Sneak Preview)*

Rascal, the cat, loved adventure. He lived for it, in fact. "I will spend 8 of my 9 lives seeking adventure," he would say. "I will save the 9$^{th}$ one for lots of catnaps and frozen Mousicles."

Well, today promised to be one of those days. He just knew that something exciting – maybe a little scary, but exciting nonetheless – was in store for him. He and his friends were deep inside a cold, dark cave. They had walked for hours through one of the most remote and heavily wooded sections of the Enchanted Forest to reach this hidden and mysterious place. Their leader for this expedition was the Prehistoric Cat named Samuel. "We will learn the history of this place in a most unusual way," he told the group of cats gathered around him. "By that, I mean we will go there and learn from real life."

The other cats meowed quietly to one another, some of them not daring to go any further. "This is the end of the line for me," said Samuel.

Rascal looked at him with wide eyes. "You are not coming with us?" he asked in surprise.

The wise old cat smiled. "No, my friends," said Samuel. "I have lived through many things already that you now need to experience for yourselves."

A bit reluctantly, but eager for adventure, Rascal said goodbye to Samuel and opened the heavy wooden door, which groaned and creaked as he pushed against it with all of his might. Carved into it, in ornate script, were the words, "Ancient Egypt – Time of the Pharaohs."

At that moment they felt the dry smell of the air and they saw a view of yellow-red sand and blue sky. The heat from this place hit them right away too, like a blast furnace.

"Drink. I want something to drink," whispered Lumby, the cute little kitten, in Bunny's ear.

"Scorpion! Look out, everyone!" screamed Snow as she leaped up into the air in fright.

The others all turned toward her voice and recoiled in horror as they saw the large spider scurry past.

"Two venomous snakes from the right side!" shouted Bunny, freezing in his tracks.

"And another one on the left" added Rascal, trying to remain calm.

"Let's go back home," said Sofia seriously.

The other cats were all agitated too, their backs arched, tails straight up in the air ready for battle.

"Do not move!" called a strange voice, like dogs barking.

The cats instantly lay down without any movement. Bunny remained frozen with his right front paw tucked up like a hunting dog, set and standing at attention.

From behind a sand dune came a small cat and in a flash he attacked the snake that was ready to bite

Rascal. Sofia, in terror, closed her eyes while Snow was breathing heavily. The snake took a terrible beating and slithered off as fast as he could, lucky to keep his skin for another season.

This strange cat said, "You are lucky that you stopped moving," and quickly hunted down and got rid of the two other snakes that were approaching from Bunny's right side. Then in a low-pitched sound, like a barking dog, the voice said, "Now I invite you all for supper."

"Holy Cat! This is a cat, not a dog!" said Rascal, surprised and looking at the tiny cat, yellow like sand.

The small cat laughed. "Right, my friend, I am indeed a cat. My name is Sand Cat."

"You are a most powerful warrior," said Philosopher, Rascal's wise brother.

"I am as I am," the humble cat replied.

"Drink! Drink! Drink! I'm thirsty!" cried Lumby.

The others chimed in, too. All of them, even in the short time they had been here, were parched. Their throats were getting dry and scratchy from the heat, not to mention the sand.

Sand Cat shook his head. "No, that is not possible right now," he said. "There is no water in this place."

"No water!" shouted the cats.

"No. I do not drink water. I do not drink at all."

"Let's go back home. I do not want to die here

without water!" implored Sofia, her face filled with dread.

The cats looked back, but the door through which they had come had vanished!

Everywhere there was only sand, sand and more sand. They were beginning to feel trapped...

**Coming Soon!**

Sign up at <u>www.netinfodirect.com</u> for updates on new cats stories by Boszenna Nowiki

**Healthy Life Press Inc.**
1733 H street suite 330 PMB 860
Blaine, WA  98230- 5107

Email: orders@netinfodirect.com
Tel. (888) 575 3173
Fax: (604) 682 5817

# BOOK ORDER FORM

Please send ____copies of the book **"Why Some Cats are Rascals"**
**at the price of:**

(Check applicable)

      [ ] $8.95 US, for the total of…….………….................. $_____

      [ ] $11.95 Canadian, for the total of……….................. $_____

Add Shipping and Handling:

(US and Canada: $3.95 for one; add $1.00 for each additional book)…………. $_____

Canadian orders add sales taxes:

      GST (7%)…………………………………………………… $_____

      BC orders add PST (7.5%)…………................... $_____

      TOTAL……………………………………………………... $_____

(Check applicable)

      [ ]  Enclosed is my check or money order or.............$_____

      [ ]  I would like to pay with my VISA.

Shipping Address          Please Print Clearly

| | |
|---|---|
| Your Name: | |
| Address: | |
| City, State/Province | |
| Zip/Postal Code: | |
| Tel/Fax  Number: | |
| Email address: | |

Please charge my **VISA** Number:

| | | | | | | | | | | | | | | | |
|---|---|---|---|---|---|---|---|---|---|---|---|---|---|---|---|
| | | | | | | | | | | | | | | | |

Expiry Date:

| | | / | | |
|---|---|---|---|---|
| | | | | |

The amount of **(Check applicable)**: [ ] $_____US [ ] _____CAD

Cardholder  name:_____

Signature: _____Date:_____